Sweet Deal

HONEYSUCKLE TEXAS ★ BOOK 4

CHRIS KENISTON

Indie House Publishing

Indie House Publishing

MORE BOOKS
By Chris Keniston

Honeysuckle Texas
Sweet Beginnings
Sweet Surprise
Sweet Temptation
Sweet Deal
Sweet Obsession
Sweet Tomorrows
Sweet Redemption

The Billionaire Barons of Texas
Just One Date
Just One Spark
Just One Dance
Just One Take
Just One Taste
Just One Shot
Just One Chance
Just One Mistake
Just One Family
Just One Rodeo
Just One Surprise
Just One Look

Hart Land
Heather
Lily
Violet
Iris
Hyacinth
Rose
Calytrix
Zinnia

Poppy
Picture Perfect

Farraday Country
Adam
Brooks
Connor
Declan
Ethan
Finn
Grace
Hannah
Ian
Jamison
Keeping Eileen
Loving Chloe
Morgan
Neil
Owen
Paxton
Quinn

Honeymoon Series
Honeymoon for One
Honeymoon for Three
Honeymoon for Four
Honeymoon for Five
Honeymoon for Six
Honeymoon for Seven

Aloha Romance Series:
Aloha Texas
Almost Paradise
Mai Tai Marriage
Dive Into You
Look of Love
Love by Design
Love Walks In
Shell Game
Flirting with Paradise

Surf's Up Flirts:
(Aloha Series Companions)
Shall We Dance
Love on Tap
Head Over Heels
Perfect Match
Just One Kiss
It Had to Be You
Cat's Meow

CHAPTER ONE

Even her mother's strong coffee wasn't quite enough to cut through the pre-dawn chill, or the bone-deep weariness Rachel Sweet felt as she stood by the kitchen window. Outside, the eastern sky was just beginning to blush pink, promising another long West Texas day. A day that would start, like all the others lately, with ranch chores before the sun was fully up, followed by a full day of her real job, the one that paid her a salary, and likely more ranch chores after that. She stifled a yawn and refilled her favorite oversized mug, the one that declared, 'World's Okayest Social Worker'. Some days, 'okayest' felt like a stretch.

The quiet shuffle of footsteps announced Jillian before she even appeared. Her twin eased into the kitchen, looking just as tired, her usual bright energy dimmed around the edges. She bypassed the coffee pot and went straight for the kettle.

"Tea morning?" Rachel took a long slow sip of the scalding coffee.

"Yeah, I need something soothing." Jillian yawned, leaning against the counter while she waited for the water to heat. "My brain is already running through candle scent combinations and inventory spreadsheets. It's hard to switch off."

"Tell me about it." Rachel looked out the window again, past the familiar shapes of the barns and paddocks just starting to emerge from the dark. "Sometimes I dream about client files and broken fences."

"Don't forget the looming threat of foreclosure," Jillian

added dryly, pouring hot water over a tea bag in her own mug.

Rachel winced. "Way to bring down the mood before sunrise."

"Sorry." Jillian sighed, joining Rachel by the window. They stood in comfortable silence for a moment, sipping their respective drinks, the shared burden hanging unspoken between them.

Swallowing the last drop, Rachel rinsed the mug and set it in the dishwasher. "I'm heading for the barn."

Doing the same, her sister turned on her heel. "Right behind you."

Already at work mucking stalls, Garret turned to face them, his expression set with the quiet determination he seemed to wear constantly these days. "Morning."

Leaning the shovel against the wall, he straightened, stretching his back.

Rachel glanced around this side of the large barn. "Where's everyone?"

"Carson and Clint are off rounding up some cattle that broke through the east fence."

"Again?" This was the second time in as many days. Rachel knew that these things happened from time to time, sometimes more often than they'd like, but two days in a row?

"What about Preston?" Jillian asked.

"Right here." Their other brother came out of the tack room. Lately he'd taken to working at the small desk in the corner of the packed room when he didn't want to take any chance of their mom stumbling onto what they were doing to save the ranch.

"I don't like that look on your face."

"It's the only one I've got." Their brother's effort at humor fell flat.

Jillian groaned softly. "I'd like to think with three weddings in the family that we'd be in a better place, but that expression doesn't scream good news."

"No, there is some good news. Thanks to Garret's contribution," Preston's gaze darted to his brother and back, "we were able to replace the main well pump for the north pastures. No doubt it probably hadn't been maintained in years."

"Nice of it to wait till Garret and Jackie were married to finally give out." Rachel half-heartedly chuckled. "So, what's the bad news?"

"While we've been able to keep up, meeting the next bank payment is going to be rough."

"I'll bite." Jillian remained focused on her brother. "How rough is rough?"

Preston blew out a long breath. "I can't make the math work."

Her brother didn't have to say the rest of the sentence out loud: unless one of the remaining single Sweets tied the knot. The unspoken pressure landed squarely back on her and Jillian. With Kade deployed overseas, unreachable for this kind of crazy scheme, it was down to them.

"Blast." Jillian kicked at the ground. "I've got nothing."

Rachel managed a weak smile. "Me neither. I haven't been able to find anyone even worth suggesting a temporary deal to, never mind being rejected because of the no sex clause."

Garret leaned back against the stall wall. "We need a solution, and it doesn't look like Prince Charming, even a temporary one, is riding in on a white horse anytime soon."

"I'm open to any brilliant ideas you might have." Jillian's tone dripped with sarcasm.

"Hey," Garret raised both his hands, palm open, "just stating the facts."

The weight settled heavier on her shoulders. Her brothers had stepped up, finding love in the most unexpected ways through this bizarre family pact. It had worked for them, against all odds. Now it was her turn, or Jillian's, or Kade's. She looked out at the sprawling land just beginning to wake under the Texas sky—the land that held generations of Sweet history, the land her father had loved, the land her mother was fighting so hard to keep. She couldn't let them lose it. She just couldn't.

The Pacific Ocean stretched out below, a vast expanse of improbable blue meeting an equally flawless sky. At a favorite seaside restaurant for everyone who was anyone, perched high on the cliffside, the view from their table was designed to impress. A daily masterpiece served alongside pricey entrees and meticulously curated wine lists. James Henderson sipped his mineral water, the condensation beading on the delicate crystal. Everything here felt polished to a high shine, including, he was beginning to realize, the life he'd built.

Across the table, Blair adjusted the cuff of her silk blouse, the diamond on her left hand catching the California sunlight in a spray of dazzling, and very expensive, fire. She tilted her head, considering the linen swatch the wedding planner had left them. "The Egyptian cotton is lovely, of course, but I think the Belgian linen has a more… substantial feel. Speaks to legacy, tradition. Don't you agree, darling?"

James nodded, his gaze drifting past her shoulder to the endless ocean. Legacy. Tradition. Here, those words seemed to translate to thread counts and import taxes. Back home, they meant two hundred years of ranchers working the same stubborn piece of Texas land, leaky barn roofs, the taunting aroma of fresh baked goods, and the easy, unpretentious laughter shared over iced tea on the porch. He hadn't thought much about Honeysuckle in years, not really, too busy chasing the California dream. And he'd caught it. After years of late nights and long weeks, his firm thrived. Emblems of success for all to see, the sleek condo overlooking the ocean, tailored clothing suitable for a king, and the beautiful fiancée planning their six-figure wedding. He had everything he thought he ever wanted. So why did it all feel so… hollow? When all was said and done, chic condos, expensive linens, and having a wedding that made the society pages wasn't much of a legacy.

"…And Henri insists that for the reception centerpieces,

only white Phalaenopsis orchids flown in that morning will do. Anything less would be... well, unthinkable," Blair continued, flipping through a glossy magazine featuring impossibly thin models draped in couture. "He assures me they have a dedicated supplier."

"Sounds expensive," James murmured, forcing his attention back.

Blair waved a dismissive hand, her bracelets chiming softly. "Quality always is, darling. We can't skimp now. Think of the photos! Think of who will be there!" She leaned forward, her eyes bright with satisfaction. "Speaking of, I think seating Mother next to Judge Harrington would be a wise move, politically."

He tried to picture his own mother navigating this landscape of social maneuvering and imported orchids. She'd probably ask where the corn bread was and if the band knew "Cotton-Eyed Joe." The image brought a faint, wistful smile to his lips. The word legacy continued to bounce around in his head.

"Did you hear me, James?" Blair's tone held a faint edge of impatience.

He searched for a plausible answer. "Sorry, just thinking about... logistics. Flying in orchids seems rife with potential complications."

She laughed, a light, brittle sound. "Darling, that's why we pay the best people to handle the complications." She reached across the table, her perfectly manicured nails tapping his hand. "It will be the wedding of the century. Every bride in the country will want a wedding like ours."

He had his doubts. Most people just wanted to live happily ever after with the love of their lives, regardless of whether or not the groom wore platinum cuff links. This wedding had become little more than a show. A carefully constructed statement of success and affluence, devoid of simple, genuine, even if often messy, connections mere mortals craved.

Memories of his youth flooded his thoughts. Summer nights spent cranking the ice cream machine on the front porch, laughing with friends in open fields, and swatting mosquitoes under a sky thick with stars, not city haze. The very things he'd once found boring and mundane suddenly seemed to be more full of life than the miles of ocean before them.

He looked at Blair, really looked at her. Beautiful, intelligent, ambitious—everything he thought he admired. Her focus was always outward—on appearances, status, the next acquisition. The perfect power couple. Except, his own focus had shifted inward, questioning the very success he'd achieved. The disconnect between them felt like a chasm.

"Blair," he began softly, interrupting her rambling chatter on whether champagne or prosecco was more appropriate for the cocktail hour.

She looked up, a slight frown creasing her smooth forehead. "Yes?"

He took a breath. "I can't do this."

"Can't do what?" Her frown deepened. "Decide on the champagne? Honestly, James, sometimes you—"

"No," he cut her off. "I mean this." He gestured widely, encompassing the restaurant, the plans, and the life they were building. "The wedding. Us."

Lips painted the perfect shade of Notice Me red formed a silent O of surprise seconds before cool eyes narrowed. "I... see. Is there someone else?" It wasn't asked with hurt, but with a kind of clinical curiosity, as if assessing a failed business deal.

"No. It's not about someone else. It's about me. This life... the one we're planning... it's beautiful, it's enviable, but it's not what I want." He sighed, his words sounding harsh to his own ears. "It's better to realize that now than years down the road." He drew the napkin from his lap and set it on the table beside him. "I'm truly sorry, Blair."

"Sorry?" Fury seemed to battle rage in her eyes, but somehow, he doubted it had anything to do with a lost love and everything to do with appearances. "What am I supposed to tell everyone?"

And there it was. Confirmation that his new reality was anything but real. Pushing to his feet and dropping cash on the table to cover the ridiculously priced water and her

untouched mimosa, he looked out at the perfect blue ocean
that matched his perfectly coifed fiancée sitting at the
perfectly set table. How had he ever let his life come to
this?

CHAPTER TWO

"Honestly?" Rachel grumbled into her phone, steering the pickup truck carefully toward town. "If I have to vet one more potential *husband* who thinks this is some kind of reality show audition, I'm going to strangle someone."

On the other end, Jillian sighed dramatically. "Tell me about it. The guy yesterday who on paper seemed to have potential, when I spoke to him wanted to know if the ranch came with mineral rights included in the one-year deal. Seriously? What we need is a miracle. And sooner than later would be good."

"Miracles are in short supply, just like suitable, sane men willing to play pretend for a year." Rolling into town, she hadn't realized she and her sister had been grumbling at each other since she'd pulled away from the ranch. Truth was that they were both beyond frustrated. Wanting so badly to help the family, to do their share, and yet, unable to find the Holy Grail their brothers had.

As she passed Corn Hole Heaven, her aunts stood near the doorway, engaged in what looked like a very serious discussion with Mildred McEntire. Who knew what that was all about? Could be anything from pricing for their blinged out corn hole products, or the price of eggs, or gossiping about some local resident caught red handed doing something to make tongues wag. Though usually the one to do all the gossiping was Iris Hathaway, Mildred could definitely hold her own.

When the women glanced in her direction, Rachel gave a quick wave. Aunt Vicki returned it with a flourish that nearly knocked over a display board. Rachel chuckled. She really did love her aunts, maybe as much as her own mother, but the Corn Hole Queens and Alice Sweet were very different.

"I should go. I've got to grab a parking spot and get through my shopping list."

"How long is the list?" Jillian asked.

"Long enough. Besides what I need, Mom is in deep clean mode. She started clearing out one of the line shacks."

"Uh-oh." Jillian's voice took on a serious tone. "That means she's worrying."

"My guess is Preston must have mentioned the upcoming payments due."

"Sounds about right. One thing's for sure, when she's done that shack will gleam."

"It will once I pick up some cleaning supplies. We ran low when she decided to reorganize the pantry after Carson mentioned the irrigation system wasn't working as needed."

"Don't remind me." Jillian heaved a sigh. "She was dusting like the Tasmanian devil until the boys reported back that it wasn't as bad as expected."

All of this was one more reason for her to hurry up and find a man. And like it or not, it was time she faced the fact that pretty much any man that was breathing would have to do. How she hated that thought. "All right. I have to run."

"If you're bored, pop in. I'm tinkering with a new scent. Something special for next month's art festival."

"No idea why you bother, your honeysuckle scents are always the bestsellers. But will do if there's time." A few quick see you laters and reminders not to buy out the store and Rachel hit the disconnect button on her truck's steering wheel then glanced toward the town park as she passed. A genuine smile touched her lips. Mason was there, racing around the green space, a gaggle of local kids running with him. Her nephew looked so completely at home, his laughter carrying over the truck's engine. One more reason why she was going to make this happen. The Sweet Legacy could not die, it had to stay strong for the next generation, for Mason.

Pulling into a parking space, she slid out of the front

seat and slammed the door. Miller's Dry Goods was one of those wonderful small-town institutions that seemed to have a little bit of everything. She quickly found the industrial-strength degreaser her mother swore by, a tub of specialty saddle soap that smelled richly of leather and beeswax, a pack of oversized sponges sturdy enough to scrub down a horse trailer, and, unable to resist, grabbed a bag of the locally roasted coffee beans Agnes used at the café. It all went into one large, slightly cumbersome brown paper grocery bag.

"Need another bag, honey?" Mrs. Miller asked from behind the counter, her spectacles perched on the end of her nose.

"No thanks, I can manage." Rachel handed over her credit card.

Bag balanced against her hip with one arm, she pushed open the heavy glass door, the bell above it jingling merrily. Outside on the sidewalk, the afternoon sun felt warm. She fumbled in her front jeans pocket with her free hand, trying to fish out her truck keys. They were, naturally, caught on her lip balm and a stray tissue. Concentrating, trying not to drop the increasingly awkward bag, she took a step away from the storefront, wrestling the keys free.

"Here, let me get that."

The voice was deep, warm, smooth as worn leather, and so startlingly familiar it sent a jolt straight through her. She looked up, keys halfway out of her pocket, and froze. Standing right beside her, reaching instinctively for the grocery bag, was a man she hadn't seen in years, a man whose easy grin hadn't changed.

Her breath caught. The keys slipped from her numb fingers, clattering onto the sidewalk. The grocery bag followed, tilting precariously. Sponges tumbled out, the bag of coffee beans landed with a soft thud, and the degreaser started a slow roll towards the curb. None of it registered. All she saw was the face she thought she'd only see in old yearbooks.

"Jimmy?" The name slipped from her lips, not quite a question, more of a reverent proclamation. Then it hit her,

Jimmy Henderson—in the flesh—was standing in front of her. A joyful laugh burst from her chest. Forgetting the spilled groceries, forgetting the ranch's troubles, forgetting everything, she launched herself forward.

Pure instinct had James wrapping his arms around the woman now plastered against him. One moment he was taking in the familiar, almost achingly quaint facade of Miller's Dry Goods, feeling the Texas sun warm his face after years under a different sky, and the next, a whirlwind of denim, flying blonde hair, and surprised green eyes hurtled towards him.

He barely had time to register what had happened and who he was now spinning around in a wide circle, taking up the entire sidewalk, when he found himself laughing, a real, deep belly laugh that felt like shaking dust off something long unused. He hadn't laughed like this, hadn't felt this jolt of pure, uncomplicated surprise and connection, in… well, longer than he cared to admit.

Her laugh was just as bright and breathless as he remembered, a sound that cut straight through the carefully constructed layers of his California success.

He slowed the spin, setting her back on her feet, though his hands lingered at her waist for a fraction of a second longer than necessary. They stood there, breathless, grinning at each other amidst a small, comical scattering of sponges and coffee beans. Her cheeks were flushed, her eyes wide with disbelief, mirroring his own.

"Rachel Sweet," he finally managed, his voice maybe a little rougher than usual.

"Jimmy Henderson." She grinned up at him.

"I go by…" he was about to say James when it struck him that he didn't want to be James anymore. He'd left James behind on the California coast. "Jim now."

"Jim," she said softly, slowly, as if deciding if she liked the way it rolled off her tongue. Her smile brightened. "It suits you. You're not a scrawny little kid anymore."

He didn't dare say neither was she. From the few moments he held her in his arms, there was little doubt that she'd grown up—and filled out—well.

Rachel took a half-step back, tucking a stray strand of hair behind her ear, her gaze dropping briefly to the spilled purchase, she bent over and began gathering the scattered items.

Immediately, he crouched down beside her. "Sorry. I didn't mean to startle you."

"You did more than that." Her grin was directed at him and struck him in the gut—hard. "I never expected to see you around here again."

He had spent most of high school daydreaming about leaving Honeysuckle in the dust. In college, his attitude hadn't changed. Once he had the sheepskin in hand, he'd moved to the coast and used his early financial gains to fly his folks out to California for the holidays.

"Can't say that I ever expected to be back." He dropped the last sponge into the bag she held.

Her forehead creased and her nose did that funny little crinkle thing he'd always found so adorable. "Is something wrong?" Her eyes widened. "Are your folks all right? I didn't hear—"

Shaking his head, he cut her off. "Mom and Dad are fine. Nothing's wrong. Unless, of course, you consider sleeping on the living room sofa bed because your parents decided to remodel the second floor wrong, all is quite well. I just felt…" what did he feel? He wasn't going to tell her that the brass ring wasn't all it was cracked up to be. "It was time to come home."

"That's nice to hear." She chuckled softly. "Except for the sofa bed part, that is."

Staring at those twinkling eyes and sweet smile, all without a lick of makeup on, he had to ask himself what he had ever seen in Blair. "I'm glad." Suddenly, she took a step in retreat and nestled the bulging bag on her hips again. He very much hoped he hadn't said something wrong. "The offer still stands?"

Her brows dipped in confusion.

"With the bag."

"Oh," the smile was back, "I think I've got it."

Having picked up the keys to her vehicle, he handed them to her. "Are you in a hurry to get back to the ranch?"

Her head shook from side to side and just like that, the simple gesture made him very happy.

"Does Agnes still make the best coffee in the state?"

"She does." Rachel juggled the bag again. "And the A La Mode still has the best homemade ice cream."

The ice cream had been their go to treat most of their youth. Not till college and long study nights did he learn to love Agnes's coffee. "Ice cream sounds even better. Care to join me?"

Rachel nodded. "Just give me a second to put this in the truck."

Standing on the curb, watching her lean into the truck and deposit her purchases, Jim felt like a teenager again. It was probably not even a little appropriate, but he couldn't miss how nicely the denim hugged her well-rounded derriere. Had she filled a pair of jeans like that when they were in school? If she had, how the heck had he missed it?

"All set." Spinning about, she slammed the door shut and smiled up at him. Still a very nice smile. "Shall we?"

With a nod, he fell into step beside her. The ice cream parlor was only a few doors down Main Street. "Butter Pecan?"

Rachel stopped short and stared up at him.

"What?"

"You remembered."

"That butter pecan is—was—your favorite ice cream flavor?"

She nodded.

"Hard to forget. It's the only flavor you ever ordered every time we came here for years."

Nodding, she continued walking. "Fair enough." A smile bloomed and she tipped her head and flashed a smile at him that made her eyes sparkle. "Pistachio?"

Another laugh escaped his throat. "Touché." He

couldn't stop smiling, and had to think hard—when was the last time he laughed so easily and so often, in only a few minutes?

CHAPTER THREE

T he rough wood of the park bench felt grounding beneath Rachel's fingertips. They'd walked the short block from A La Mode in a surprisingly comfortable silence, the ice cream cones a relic of their easier, younger days. Now, sitting here under the shade of a sprawling oak, the real world, with all its current complications, seemed miles away. Beside her, Jimmy attacked his pistachio ice cream with a focus that made her smile. They had been such good friends. Ever since Ben Fabio had intentionally tripped her in the hallway in eighth grade and then a few feet down the hall, Jimmy had nonchalantly stood by his locker, stuck his foot out at just the right moment and sent Ben tumbling to the ground landing with a loud splat against the linoleum floor. Smiling at her as she brushed herself off, he winked, made her giggle, and from that moment on, she and Jimmy had been best buds.

"So," Jim leaned back against the bench, "catch me up on the Sweets."

Rachel laughed. "How long have you been back in town?"

His gaze dropped to the dripping ice cream cone in his hand. "Today is my first full day. I got into town late yesterday afternoon."

"Mm hm. And you mean to tell me that your mother hasn't caught you up on all the comings and goings in Honeysuckle?"

A deep chuckle rattled in his chest. "Well, maybe a little."

"How little?"

"The aunts are doing great with Corn Hole Heaven and

doing more than their share to keep Honeysuckle on the tourist map. Three of your brothers have recently gotten married."

"Correct."

"Like within a few months of each other."

She nodded.

"I have to ask—did someone spike the well water?"

This was one of the things she missed about Jimmy—Jim. He could always make her laugh over the simplest of things. If only he knew. "Something like that."

"I hear everyone's moved back to the ranch?"

Once upon a time they'd told each other almost everything, but that was a very long time ago. Now, she debated how much to tell him. A loyalty to forever ago friendship won the debate. "We lost our foreman several months ago and we all agreed to move home and help Mom. It was hard on all of us losing Dad, but running the ranch alone is too much for her."

"I'm sorry. Mom told me when Charlie passed. I sent a note with flowers. Wanted to call, but," he sighed, "something always got in the way of my good intentions."

"I got the letter. It was lovely. So were the flowers."

For a long moment, they licked the ice cream and sat in the somber silence.

"I meant to stay better in touch," he blurted. "I don't know what happened. What is it they say: life is what happens while we're busy making other plans?"

"Sounds like something my Grandma Davis would have said."

"It's true." He crunched on the end of his cone. "I really am sorry. I should have made the time to call, to—"

"Hey," she put her hand on his arm, "I didn't do any better. Not after the first year or so." She'd missed her friend so much back then. They'd talk often at first, then the calls grew distant; soon she hadn't even noticed that they weren't coming at all.

He tossed the napkin into a nearby trash can. "Mom says you're still doing social work."

"I am." Her cheeks pulled at the corner of her mouth.

"I'm gathering from that wide grin that it's turned out to be all you'd hoped it would?"

"For the most part, yes." She took a quick nibble at the edge of her cone. "Folks like me live for the next crisis, the next problem to solve. We love fixing wrongs."

"And when you can't?" The man really did know her too well.

"That's the not most part. It's hard. Sometimes more than others, but any social worker knows going into a situation, we can't save everyone. We can only do our best."

"But you like your job?"

There were also people, kids, and families, that she couldn't help, others like the Bensons that broke her heart, but that didn't change the facts. "Love it."

He studied her with an intensity she didn't quite understand. Years ago, she would have known exactly what he was thinking, but not anymore. The tall lanky kid who had been her partner in crime had left town a long time ago. This man in front of her, with broad shoulders, subtle strength, and a killer smile that made his blue eyes sparkle like the Caribbean on a sunny day, was practically a stranger.

The distant sounds of children playing and birds calling in the trees above filled the quiet air that had settled around them.

"So," she ventured, "how long are you staying in Honeysuckle?"

Jim tilted his head, considering. "I don't know yet."

"When do you have to be back to work?"

"I don't."

She felt her brows slowly ride high on her forehead. "You lost your job?"

He shook his head.

"Then you must have one heck of a great boss." Though she didn't know why that statement made him chuckle.

"That depends." He shrugged, still smiling. "I'm the boss."

"Ah." She nodded. "I don't remember your mother

mentioning that. Though I admit, we don't talk often."

"I'm surprised she didn't shout from the rooftops every time I moved up the corporate ladder."

"She might have if I'd still been living in town, but I only moved back recently, like the others, to help Mom." There were so many things she wanted to ask him, so many years she wanted to catch up on, and yet, sitting here side by side, even though she didn't have a clue what was going on in his life, somehow, she felt as if no time at all had passed. How was that even possible?

Jim watched Rachel finish her ice cream cone, the tip of her tongue catching a stray drop of butter pecan. He had to physically stop himself from leaning closer. *Love it*. The simple conviction in her voice when she spoke about her job resonated deep within him. Until recently, he would have said the same thing about his work. The risks, the challenges, the triumphs, and, of course, the profits. He doubted that Rachel would wake up one day and feel her work was all—superficial.

Thinking back, the passionate streak he could hear in her voice had always been there. The desire to fix things, whether it was a wobbly birdhouse in her backyard or, apparently, the more complex problems of the families she worked with now. It was admirable. It was... Rachel. "Takes guts dealing with the tough stuff day in and day out."

She shrugged, though a faint blush touched her cheeks. "Comes with the territory. You learn to focus on the wins, however small." She crumpled her napkin and aimed for the nearby trash can, missing by an inch. "Almost," she muttered, getting up to retrieve it.

He chuckled. "Some things never change. Remember trying to teach you to skip rocks at the creek? You had more enthusiasm than accuracy."

Rachel sat back down, laughing. "Hey! I got pretty

good—eventually. Unlike some people who insisted on trying to build a raft out of driftwood and nearly floated halfway to Miller's Creek before Garret lassoed them back."

"Okay, first," Jim held up a finger, grinning, "that raft was structurally sound, mostly. Second, Garret only showed up because you tattled."

"Did not!" She swatted playfully at his arm. "I merely expressed concern for your safety to the nearest responsible adult-adjacent person, who happened to be my brother with a rope."

"Semantics." He laughed, the sound feeling easy and unfamiliar in his own ears. How long had it been since he'd felt this light, this unburdened? Sitting here, trading childhood stories with Rachel Sweet, felt more real, more right, than any power lunch or boardroom meeting ever had. He'd come home seeking… something. He hadn't expected that something might be connected to the place he'd tried so hard to escape.

In passing, she casually mentioned having missed their friendship. He had too, until this very moment, more than he'd realized. "You know," his tone turned slightly more serious, "leaving Honeysuckle felt like the only option back then. College, career… it all seemed to point away from here." He looked around the familiar park—the ancient oak spreading its branches, the worn patches of grass where countless kids had played, the faint scent of honeysuckle drifting on the breeze. "Funny how you can achieve everything you thought you wanted and realize the view from the top isn't all it's cracked up to be. Sometimes the things you run away from are the things you needed all along."

Rachel studied him, her green eyes thoughtful. "Want to tell me about it?"

"Not much to tell. Didn't take me long to figure out that in the world of finance, hedge funds was a prime sector for making money—serious money. I set out to do just that."

"Judging by those loafers you're wearing, and that you mentioned you're the boss, looks like you succeeded."

"So it seems." He'd packed a single bag with the most basic casual attire he owned, but if he didn't want to be judged by his shoes, it might be good for him to get some new duds. "Or maybe success, like beauty, is in the eye of the beholder." And looking at her, seeing the genuine warmth in her smile, the intelligence shining in her eyes, he had a sudden, startlingly clear idea of how petty his interpretation had been.

His gaze drifted over her shoulder towards the dedicated corn hole courts at the far end of the park, bustling even on a weekday afternoon. He remembered the town's obsession, the tournaments, the endless summer evenings spent tossing bags with his brothers. It was part of the fabric of this place, something he hadn't thought about in ages, maybe not at all.

A shout from across the park caught their attention. A golden retriever had stolen a Frisbee from another dog and raced in victory circles around the grass, both owners in pursuit.

"Five bucks says the retriever makes at least three more laps before they catch him," Jim challenged, grateful for the distraction from his inner thoughts.

Rachel's competitive spirit flashed in her eyes. "You're on. I say they grab him before he completes two."

They both leaned forward, elbows on knees, watching intently as the canine drama unfolded. The retriever darted between a young couple having a picnic, sending a bowl of chips flying, then sprinted toward the playground with both owners in pursuit.

"That's one lap." Jim grinned.

"Just wait," Rachel countered. "See the kid by the swings with the hot dog? Ten seconds and that dog is stopping for a snack."

Sure enough, the retriever skidded to a halt beside a young boy holding a hot dog. The boy's mother snatched the food away just in time, but the pause was enough for the retriever's owner to dive forward, missing the dog but managing to grab the Frisbee.

"Ha!" Rachel crowed as the retriever, without his prize,

circled back to his owner's side. "Less than two laps, as predicted."

"Technicality," Jim protested. "They caught the Frisbee not the dog."

"Nope. Rules are rules, Henderson." She held out her hand, wiggling her fingers. "Pay up."

Laughing, Jim dug into his pocket and pulled out a five-dollar bill, pressing it into her palm. Their fingers touched, and for a brief moment, neither moved. Pulling in a deep breath, he drew his hand away and shifted in place. "You always could read a situation better than me."

Her expression unreadable, she folded the bill carefully and tucked it into her shirt pocket. "Social worker, remember? Reading people is my superpower."

"And fixing them your kryptonite," he teased, remembering how even as kids, she'd always tried to solve everyone's problems.

"And that, Mr. Henderson, is why I love what I do."

"I can see that." He smiled and children's laughter reached his ears, sparking an idea. "You know, I haven't played a decent game of corn hole since I left Texas." He stood up, offering her his hand. "How about we see if either of us remembers how to actually get a bag on the board? And maybe," he smiled wider, "I might even win back my five dollars."

CHAPTER FOUR

The challenge hung in the air between them; playful and so quintessentially Jim that Rachel couldn't help the laugh that bubbled up. Win his five dollars back at corn hole? It was like stepping back decades, to a time when their biggest worries involved navigating high school hallways and finding creative ways to beat each other at everything from skipping rocks to arcade games. It felt easy. It felt normal. It felt… surreal.

She let him pull her to her feet, the warmth of his hand lingering even after he let go. Her gaze did a quick, involuntary scan from his perfectly combed hair down to his ridiculously impractical shoes. Expensive tasseled loafers. In the heart of West Texas cattle country. Oh, this wouldn't do. Not at all.

A mischievous grin she couldn't contain spread across her face. She deliberately looked him up and down again, slowly this time, letting her amusement show. "Planning on beating me at corn hole dressed like that, Henderson?" She gestured pointedly towards his feet. "I hate to break it to you, but that buttery leather, nice as it is, won't survive five minutes on an unpaved surface.

He glanced down at his shoes, then back at her, a flicker of something in his gaze—maybe surprise, maybe embarrassment—quickly replaced by that easy grin. "They're comfortable."

"Comfortable for closing million-dollar deals, maybe. Not so much for actual real life."

"Closing deals isn't real life?" He did his best to put on a stern expression, but the twinkle in his eyes gave away the humor he was hiding.

"That's right. And don't even get me started on those slacks." She waved a hand dismissively. "You can't possibly be of any use to your family, or muck about the corn hole courts looking like you're about to attend a yacht club luncheon."

He ran a hand through his hair, the gesture endearingly familiar despite the years. "Point taken. Problem is... I don't actually have any jeans or boots here that still fit."

She burst out laughing again. James Henderson, successful California businessman, back in his hometown without a single pair of functional jeans. It stripped away some of the intimidating polish, making him feel less like a visitor from another planet and more like the slightly clueless friend she remembered.

Shaking her head in mock disbelief, she settled her hands on her hips and tipped her head at him. "What happened to the Texas boy I knew?"

"Apparently, he got temporarily distracted by sunshine and stock options." Jim fell easily into their old rhythm of banter. "Figured I could sort out the wardrobe later."

An idea took hold. "Well, later is now. Consider this your official Honeysuckle Welcome Wagon intervention, conducted by yours truly." She hooked her thumb back towards the shops lining Main Street. "Forget corn hole for a minute. First mission: Operation Find Jim Some Real Clothes. We need to get you into a decent pair of jeans that look like they might actually encounter dirt occasionally, and boots that won't dissolve if they step in something... organic." She started walking towards the street, glancing back over her shoulder, enjoying the slightly bewildered look on his face. "Unless, of course, you're worried a little denim and leather might cramp your sophisticated California style?"

He hesitated for only a second before that familiar laugh rumbled out and he fell into step beside her, easily matching her stride. "I'm all yours."

All yours. Loaded words if ever she'd heard any. It took a few moments to drag her mind back from places they should most definitely not go. Her job was to get this guy some decent work clothes so he didn't stick out like a sore city boy's thumb, not to let her imagination run wild with what she could do if he really were *all hers*.

Tempted to link arms or hold hands as they walked down the street, Rachel decided keeping her hands in her pocket was the safe move. "Miller's General Store has expanded some since you lived here. The pet shop next door went out of business about ten years ago and they took up the space. They've got a pretty good selection of clothing now. Both work wear and even party clothes."

"No more having to drive to Miller's Creek for church clothes?" he teased.

"Nope." She slowed her steps as they drew closer to the shop. "But if you want, we can buy some of those for you too."

For the umpteenth time since they bumped into each other, they both laughed from somewhere deep down inside and Rachel felt lighter than she'd felt in ages. All their troubles, and there were many, fell away. At least for now.

Standing under the store sign, Jim shook his head. "I can't believe I'm doing this."

"Think of it as reconnecting with your roots." Rachel pushed open the door, setting off the small bell above it. "Besides, you might actually enjoy being comfortable again."

"I'm perfectly comfortable."

"You won't be the first day your dad pulls you out of bed to help muck the stalls or fix a fence post."

"There is that." He grabbed the door, ushering her inside first.

The familiar scent of leather and denim welcomed her as they stepped into the clothing side of the general store. Amy Miller, whose family had founded the place about the same time as Honeysuckle came to be, looked up from the counter and patting the gray-haired chignon behind her head, broke into a wide smile.

"Rachel Sweet. Just the person I wanted to see. That dress you—" Amy's words died on her lips as she caught sight of Jim. "Well, I'll be. Jimmy Henderson, is that you hiding under all that city polish?"

Jim's expression shifted from resigned to genuinely pleased. "Amy. It's been a while."

"Ten years at least." Amy came around the counter, giving him a quick once-over. "And from the looks of things, you need my help desperately."

Rachel laughed at the alarm that flashed across Jim's face. "That's exactly what I told him."

Amy's eyes twinkled with mischief. "Let me guess. Rachel's refusing to be seen with you until we fix…" she gestured at his entire outfit, "all of this."

"Something like that," Jim admitted.

"Well, you've come to the right place." Amy clapped her hands together. "I'm thinking boot-cut jeans, a couple of good work shirts, and definitely proper boots."

"Yes, ma'am." Outnumbered, Jim seemed to steel himself for the inevitable.

There was something oddly satisfying about seeing Mr. California Finance surrendering to the return to his Texas roots.

His glance landed on a particularly ornate belt buckle display and for just a minute she thought he might turn tail and run.

"Shall we take the first step in your re-introduction to living in West Texas?"

A sly grin teasing one side of his mouth and he nodded. "Be gentle with me."

She almost swallowed her tongue. Did he have any idea how that sounded? Had they teased like that when they were younger, and she just hadn't noticed? Or is this what playful banter became when you were all grown up? Or maybe, just maybe, she needed that husband more than she realized. Her eyes almost rolled back into her head at her own thoughts. This was not the time to think about the fate of the ranch and her duty to save it. This was just old friends hanging out. And if anyone believed that baloney, for five dollars she had some beachfront property in Kansas to sell dirt-cheap.

The general store smelled exactly the same as it had when Jim was a kid—leather, cotton, and that peculiar mix of metal and wood that reminded him of his father's workshop. Jim ran his hand over a shelf of folded jeans, the familiar stiff denim had nothing in common with the tailored slacks hanging in his California closet.

"These," Rachel declared, pulling a pair of dark blue Wranglers from the stack. She handed him a couple of shirts to take into the dressing room with the pants.

Jim stood in front of the three-way mirror, turning slightly. The jeans fit perfectly—comfortable, sturdy. The simple clothing shouldn't have felt like a revelation, but somehow, they did. In California, his clothes had been armor—designed to impress, to fit in, to project an image of success and sophistication. Here, that armor felt unnecessary. Cumbersome, even.

"You decent in there?" Rachel called.

"Define 'decent,'" he shot back, pulling aside the curtain with a flourish.

Leaning against a display rack, arms crossed, a small, genuine smile played on Rachel's lips. Not teasing, not laughing, just… watching him. Her gaze held an intensity that had nothing to do with critiquing his new wardrobe. It was the same look he'd caught a few times at the park, a look that made him feel seen in a way he hadn't felt in years, maybe ever. It sent an unexpected warmth spreading through his veins. "You clean up nice."

"It feels right." He turned to the mirror again, surprised by how true his words were.

"Okay." Amy hurried over with a pair of dark brown, basic, intended for work not show, cowboy boots. "These should do the trick. Oiled leather, good solid heel. Won't fall apart the first time you step in…" she paused, glancing at Rachel with a conspiratorial wink, "…mud."

He sat on the small bench to try them on, pulling off the ridiculous loafers and feeling like he was shedding another layer of pretense along with them. The boots felt solid, grounding. He stood up, testing his weight. No surprise, they felt right. Like coming home, they'd need a little breaking in, but before he knew it, everything would fit perfectly.

"Well?" Rachel pushed away from the rack, walking towards him. Her earlier amusement was gone, replaced by that same thoughtful scrutiny. "What's the verdict?"

He met her gaze, holding it. So many thoughts ran through his mind. "You done good. Thanks for the, uh, intervention."

"Anytime." Her voice was softer now.

Amy reappeared, triumphantly holding the ornate belt buckle he'd eyed earlier. "Almost forgot the finishing touch. Every respectable Texas man needs a statement buckle."

Before he could protest, Rachel stepped forward. "Actually, Amy, I think this one suits him better." She held up a simpler, cleaner buckle from the display—brushed silver, classic western engraving, solid without being flashy. She showed it to him. "What do you think?"

He took it, the metal cool against his palm. It was more him. Or at least, more the him he wanted to be now. How did she know that after all these years? He looked from the buckle to her face, catching that flicker of something deep and knowing in her eyes again.

"Perfect." He handed the buckle and his credit card to Amy. "Ring it all up."

"Do you want to change back into your other clothes, or should I bag them up for you?"

He shook his head. "I'll wear these. You can bag... no, you know what? Just donate them."

Amy's gaze darted over to the dressing room where his California clothes hung, and thousand-dollar leather loafers rested. She was probably wondering who the heck around here would need those, but with a gentle nod, smiled up at him and hurried back to the counter.

Standing at the register, in comfortable silence, waiting for Amy to ring up the sale, he wasn't thinking about hedge funds or bottom lines or profit ratios. He wasn't thinking about the life he'd walked away from, or the possessions he'd left in California. He was feeling more himself, more grounded, and more real than he had in over a decade.

Sale complete, credit card back in his wallet, he opened the shop door for Rachel, and standing on the curb, turned to face her. "So, am I suitable for a game of corn hole now?"

Turning her wrist, she glanced at her watch and her bright smile slipped. "I'm sorry. It's getting late and Mom is expecting me back. Rain check?"

Doing his best to hold his own smile, he nodded. "Of course. My folks are probably wondering where the heck I am too."

They stood awkwardly for another moment or two before one of them, he wasn't sure which, finally took a step back, putting distance between them.

"You won't be a stranger now, will you?" Her voice was softer, almost timid.

"Not a chance," were the only words he could form that made any sense. "I have a rain check coming."

And on that, she laughed again, pushed to her tippy toes, gave him a kiss on the cheek and hurried back to where her truck was parked.

Of all the things he'd done wrong in his life, now more than even yesterday, he was absolutely positive coming home had not been one of them.

CHAPTER FIVE

Charlie Sweet's office was the one place in the house that usually grounded Rachel. Tonight, though, it felt heavy, thick with unspoken tension. She leaned back in her favorite chair, the one that surrounded her like a warm hug, watching Preston with a sheaf of printouts clutched in his hand. His wife Sarah Sue leaned against the wet bar, a pained expression on her face as she watched her husband pace.

Across the room, Carson and Jess sat close together on the small sofa, a silent testament to their unlikely success story. Beside her, Jillian fidgeted, tapping a nervous rhythm on the armrest. Even Garret and Jackie seemed less relaxed than usual, their easy affection underscored by a shared seriousness. They were all here, the full contingent minus Kade, waiting for the other shoe to drop.

Preston finally stopped pacing and sighed, dropping the papers onto the desk. "Okay, brief update," he began, his voice tight. "Still pinched financially. We knew the three trust payments wouldn't be a magic bullet, but even without ranch hand salaries, operating expenses are still eating through the little income we're getting." He shook his head. "Basically, we're like a pack of dogs, running in circles, chasing their tails." He met each of their gazes. "We're looking at a significant shortfall again. I've tried everything I can think of, borrowing from Peter to pay Paul, and I still can't make the math work. And this afternoon," he sighed, "the hay bailer croaked. Clint was working on it a bit ago, but this is beyond juggling. We need another miracle."

A collective sigh seemed to ripple through the room. Another miracle. Otherwise known as another wedding.

Rachel's stomach twisted. The weight landed squarely, heavily, on her and Jillian.

"Right," Preston continued, running a hand through his hair. "Before we brainstorm, Kade is finally somewhere he can talk, and I promised I'd loop him in." Quickly he initiated a video call on the computer screen.

A moment later, Kade's face filled the screen now turned to face the people in the room. Their brother looked tired but smiled. "Hey! Good timing, was just about to hit the rack."

"Hey, bro," Preston greeted him. Quick pleasantries were exchanged—inquiries about his deployment—though Rachel had no idea why they bothered asking as he was never at liberty to say—reassurances were given about how Mom was holding up well considering the circumstances, and, of course, updates shared on their new nephew Mason's latest antics. Then Preston gave him the financial rundown, keeping it direct but maybe slightly less panicked than he'd sounded moments before. "Bottom line, Kade, margins are still razor thin. We're managing, but we desperately need more breathing room."

Kade's expression tightened with familiar frustration. "Wish I could do more from over here. Feels useless just watching."

"You being safe is what matters," Carson interjected firmly. Then, almost as an aside, he added, "Speaking of watching, you'll never guess who blew back into Honeysuckle. Jimmy Henderson."

Kade's eyebrows shot up. "Seriously? What in the world brought him back? Last I heard he was wiping the West Texas dust off his boots and never coming back."

"More like Italian loafers," Jillian muttered not quite under her breath.

"So, he's doing well?" Kade's expression shifted to something teetering on curiosity and approval.

"The gossip mill hasn't come around to give us all the details yet," Jillian teased, "but he certainly is looking good."

Rachel felt her cheeks warm inexplicably. She busied

herself by examining a non-existent piece of lint on her jeans.

"Hm," Kade mused. "I guess never say never."

"You spent a good amount of time with him today." Preston faced his sister. "Got anything to enlighten us?"

Rachel forced a casual shrug, avoiding looking directly at the screen. "All I know is he's taking time off from his company."

"*His* company?" Kade whistled.

"Told ya," Jillian leaned forward, "grapevine didn't have many details, but everyone agreed his attire cost more than most people's monthly income."

"Good for him." Kade bobbed his head, not quite smiling. Not that he wasn't probably happy for Jim, they just had a lot more important things on their mind right now. "Guess Honeysuckle is turning out its share of success stories. I saw that Blake Kirby is doing a European tour."

"Has a new hit on the radio too," Carson said. "Definitely living the high life."

Rachel shifted her attention to her sister who kept surprisingly silent. In the early years of Blake's music, Jillian followed his career closely. The first time one of his songs hit the top of the charts, the way Jillian carried on, anyone would have thought she had penned the tune, entitling her to an income. For all Rachel knew, Jillian might still have a thing for the guy, but if she did, she never said a word.

The conversation shifted back to general chit-chat and minor updates about the stock, the barn, and the lone ranch hand before Kade needed to sign off so he could give his mother a quick call before it was time for lights out. As soon as the screen went dark, Jillian let out an explosive sigh and turned directly to Rachel, a speculative, almost predatory gleam in her eye that Rachel instantly distrusted.

Heaving a deep sigh, Preston pushed to his feet. "We've spun our wheels long enough for one night. I vote we table this discussion until after we've all had a good night's sleep."

Garret nodded. "Maybe I'll play the lotto tomorrow."

Everyone knew he was joking, but somehow, Rachel

wasn't sure that it might not be a good idea. At least she could afford the price of one ticket.

The room emptied, but Jillian remained in her seat, swirling a glass of Ginger Ale in front of her.

"Coming?" Rachel stood by her sister's chair.

"I'm thinking." Her sister's gaze lifted to meet hers. "What about Jim?"

"What about him?" She did her best to feign ignorance, but she knew exactly where her sister was going with this.

"He's single. He's handsome. He's home. And did I mention he's single?"

"Don't be ridiculous. He lives in California. He has a business in California. He will probably visit for a bit, get his fill of West Texas dust, and then remember why he left in the first place and run home to his closet full of Italian loafers and tailored apparel."

"Or," Jill stood, "in the name of friendship, he might be willing to help us out. Y'all were awfully close once upon a time." She took a few steps and stopped by the open door. "At least think about it."

Her sister disappeared into the hallway and Rachel was left standing, her mind reeling, her jaw hanging open, and her palms starting to sweat. Could Jillian's lame idea actually work?

The low rumble of conversation, punctuated by the clink of ice in glasses and the soft thwack of cards hitting the felt-topped table, was a familiar sound. Jim nursed a lukewarm beer he didn't really want and tried to focus on the hand he'd just been dealt. Useless. Just like his concentration had been since leaving Rachel earlier that afternoon.

His brother, Mark, had practically dragged him out of their parents' house after dinner. "Come on, Jim," he'd insisted. "Wednesday night poker game at Bill's garage. Best way to reconnect with the guys, hear the real local news."

So here he was, surrounded by faces he'd known most of his life—ranchers, small business owners, guys who had stayed while he'd chased success elsewhere. The conversation flowed easily around him—complaints about the price of feed, praise for the high school quarterback's performance this season, speculation about the Friday night's upcoming game. It was the comfortable rhythm of small-town life he hadn't realized he missed.

"I'm in." Jim tossed a chip in the pot.

Mark gave him a sideways glance. "You already anted up."

"Oh." He chuckled. "Guess it's been a long day." Long didn't begin to cover it. Seeing Rachel again, spending hours just talking and laughing like no time had passed… if he thought he was confused when he walked out of that oceanside restaurant having broken his engagement to a woman he had no business marrying, he was even more confused now.

His brother eyed him a moment longer before nodding. "How was your afternoon with Rachel?"

"Rachel?" Bill looked up from his cards. "You saw her today?"

Three heads turned in his direction. Mark shook his head. "The whole town knows they ran into each other today. How the heck did you miss it?"

Shifting his cards, Bill shrugged. "Unlike some people, I actually work hard for a living."

There was no arguing that ranching was a tough job. Up before dawn, hard labor all day, and then early to bed to start over again the next day.

"Two cards." Jim tried to redirect the conversation away from Rachel.

Bill dealt him the two requested cards.

"I ran into Garret and his wife the other day. Still can't believe he's married. One minute he was our fifth player and the next he was head over boot heels in love and married."

"Don't forget Preston and Carson," Bill added. "Three weddings in only a few months. They're making the rest of us look bad."

Laughter went around the table. Jim managed a tight smile. He remembered Rachel mentioning her brothers' recent marriages back at the park. He pictured her face when she talked about them, the easy affection mixed with that undercurrent of… something else. Stress? Worry? He hadn't been able to place it then, and he couldn't now. What was really going on over at the Sweet Ranch? She'd mentioned losing their foreman, everyone moving home to help her mom. It sounded like Charlie Sweet was missed more than they were letting on.

He thought back to their afternoon. The way she'd laughed when he almost tripped retrieving her napkin at the park. The intensity in her eyes when she talked about her social work, her passion for "fixing wrongs." And the way she'd looked picking out that belt buckle for him at Miller's. Then there was that brief kiss on the cheek before she left… simple, friendly, yet it had sent a jolt through him he still felt hours later.

The pile of chips center table was growing.

"I'll call." Mark tossed a few chips onto the pile and, smiling, laid down his cards. "Three Jacks."

One by one the others tossed the cards on the table and grumbled. Jim did the same, his cards falling face up.

His brother stared at the cards. "Jim?"

"Yeah."

"You've got three aces. You should have won this round."

Blinking, he looked down at the cards. His brother was right; his mind was most definitely not on the game. Pushing back from the table, he stood. "Like I said, long day. Deal me out this hand. Need to stretch my legs. Be right back."

He stepped out of the brightly lit garage into the cool night air. The vast Texas sky arched overhead, ablaze with stars, a sight he rarely saw on the light-polluted California coast. He pulled out his phone, scrolling through his contacts, halting at Rachel Sweet, wondering if after all these years she still had the same number. Only one way to find out. Tapping the number before he had time to change his mind, he sucked in a deep breath, ran his hand behind his neck and listened to the ringing from his phone.

It rang twice before she picked up, her voice slightly breathless, "Hello."

"Hey, Rach," he tried to sound casual, leaning against the side of the house. "Didn't wake you or interrupt anything important, did I?"

"No, I was in the kitchen and my phone was upstairs."

"Sorry about that."

"No big deal." He could hear her lower the volume on a television.

All he could think was if she was in the living room or her room, then he shook his head as if chasing away the thoughts. It didn't matter.

"What are you up to?"

"Mark dragged me to a poker game at Billy's."

"Sounds like fun."

"It's nice reconnecting." That part was mostly true. "But I was thinking about that rain check."

"Still angling to win that five dollars back, Henderson?" He could almost hear her smile through the phone.

"You know it." Relief washing over him, a smile took over his face. This felt easy. Right. "Seriously, though, you busy tomorrow? Figured we could finally settle that corn hole score. Unless you'd rather do something else?"

"Oh, uh…"

His smile slipped. He shouldn't have presumed she'd be free on a weekday, or any day for that matter. They really hadn't gotten into personal details. For all he knew, she had a boyfriend. "Sorry, I forgot tomorrow's a workday."

"No. That's fine, it's just that I need to check on a family tomorrow. But I should be home late afternoon, if that'll work for you?"

"Sounds perfect." Oddly enough, it really did.

CHAPTER SIX

Thankful that rural roads were pretty much empty outside of town, Rachel raced home. Her day had not gone as planned, but somehow that wasn't unexpected. Sometimes the system simply didn't work in favor of those who most needed it. For the Bensons, today had been one of those days. Shaking her head, she forced the case details aside.

She pressed a little harder on the accelerator. She was already running late to meet Jim. A small smile touched her lips despite the lingering tension from her visit. She was actually looking forward to this evening, to the playful banter, to simply forgetting about the real world for a couple of hours.

Turning onto the long gravel drive leading up to the Sweet Ranch house, she saw a truck stopping near the front porch. Had to be Jim. Perfect timing. Sliding her car beside his, she killed the engine and hopped out.

He leaned against his truck, looking effortlessly good in the new jeans and a simple gray t-shirt, his arms crossed. His gaze drifted down to where her car stopped less than a foot from his rear bumper. That easy grin fell into place. "Cutting it a little close there, Sweet?"

"Never." She did her best to return the easy grin, but she was still too tied up in the day. "Give me five minutes to wash away the day's dust."

"Take ten." His smile softening slightly, his blue eyes seemed to hold a hint of understanding. "I'll wait right here. Can't wait to see the look on your face when I beat you."

"Keep dreaming, Henderson," she shot back over her shoulder, hurrying inside.

True to her word, maybe seven minutes later, feeling slightly more human after washing the day's grime and stress from her face, and tossing on a lightweight cotton sundress, she rejoined him on the porch, a little surprised her mother or siblings hadn't noticed him waiting. At least this way they stood a better chance of a clean escape. "Okay, ready to face defeat?"

He chuckled, opening the passenger door of his truck for her. "After you."

Settling in, she buckled up, taking note that the vehicle was in much better shape than the typical ranch truck.

"It's Mom's."

Had he read her mind?

"Made me think, if I'm going to stick around for a bit, it might be good to buy four wheels that doesn't smell inside like hay and horses."

"Are you? Going to stick around?"

"Don't know yet."

She nodded. It was none of her business what he did with his life. Besides, her day had been long enough; she was not going to add something else to her growing list of real-life worries.

"You okay?"

Blinking, she realized he'd been talking, and her mind had been wandering anywhere but here. "Sorry. Just… processing the long day."

"Tough one?" His voice was low, gentle, inviting confidence without demanding it.

Leaning her head back against the headrest, she sighed. "They're all tough in their own way. Case management in a rural setting involves home visits. When I was in the city, if my case was out on the street smoking crack, then that's where I went. Wherever I'm needed, that's where I go."

"Saving the world." There was no teasing, no sarcasm—if anything, she thought she heard a note of pride in his voice.

"I wish." She shook her head, not wanting to burden him with the details, and forced what she hoped was a convincing smile. "No more talk about my job. Tonight's sole mission is watching me utterly destroy you at corn hole."

He glanced at her again, a flicker of controlled amusement. "We'll see about that."

The deliberate shift worked. The knot in her chest eased slightly, replaced by the familiar spark of playful competition. He parked near the town's bustling corn hole courts, the scent of grilled onions and popcorn drifting on the evening air. "By any chance, are you as hungry as I am?"

A deep laugh ruptured the evening air. "Of course, I am. Men are always hungry. Even if we're not, we're like dogs, put food in front of us and we'll eat."

Two minutes later they were seated on a nearby bench, and she devoured her hot dog as if she hadn't eaten in a week. At one point, a drop of mustard lingered at the corner of Jim's mouth and unable to resist, she reached up and swiped it away with her thumb, resisting the urge to lean in and kiss the remaining dollop away.

"I guess you can dress me up but can't take me anywhere." His gaze lingered on her lips for a moment, and she wondered if he was thinking the same thing or if she merely had mustard on her lips too. Shaking his head, he stared at the last bite of his hot dog. "Know what this reminds me of?"

"A baseball game?" She bit into her last bite.

"Field day, the year before I moved away."

There had been so many field days. Her mind wandered back to the last one.

"Our deal."

"Deal?" Frowning, she fast-forwarded through her memories and then it struck her.

"You do remember?"

"If we make it to over thirty and aren't married." She couldn't spit out the rest of the words.

"That's the one. We were in quite the mood. Foot races, tug of war, hot dogs, and the silliest deal ever made."

"Right. Silly." She forced a laugh. "Oh well." Tossing the dirty wrapper and used napkin into the nearby trashcan, she turned to face him, ignoring the stupid deal that hit a little too close to home at the moment. "Ready, or do you just want to concede now?"

Pushing to his feet, he reached for her hand. "Fat chance."

Hand still tingling slightly where his had been, Rachel followed Jim toward the nearest open court. The familiar thump-thump of bean bags hitting wood filled the air, along with easy laughter and competitive calls from neighboring games. It felt good to be here, with Jim.

"Okay, Henderson," she said, grabbing a set of bright red bean bags while he claimed the blue. "Standard rules? First to 21?"

"You got it, Sweet." He grinned, hefting a blue bag. "Ladies first."

She rolled her eyes but stepped up to the line. Her first toss felt rusty, landing just short of the board with a soft puff in the dust. "No worries. I'm just getting warmed up."

Jim's first throw sailed smoothly, landing squarely on the board near the back edge. "Like riding a bike," he teased.

Her next throw was better. They traded throws, the bags landing on, off, sometimes surprisingly close to the hole. The easy rhythm of the game, the back-and-forth teasing, felt incredibly natural. With every toss, her aim improved.

"Three points for me," Jim announced as one of his bags dropped neatly through the hole.

"Lucky shot." Rachel lined up her own throw, focused, swung her arm smoothly, and watched as her red bag arch perfectly, landing dead center and sliding straight in. "And that," she dusted off her hands with mock seriousness, "makes five in a row. Gotcha."

A triumphant gleam lit up Rachel's emerald eyes. Jim couldn't help but grin. She wasn't just good; she was scary good. He had half expected her game to be rustier than his—after all, neither had the time to play the way they did when they were kids.

Having tossed the blue bags into the designated container, retrieving a five-dollar bill from his wallet, he pressed into her palm. "This is getting to be a habit."

"Isn't it, though?" She beamed, tucking the bill into her front pocket.

"Do you need to get back to the ranch, or are you up for a cup of coffee and maybe dessert?"

"I'm always up for a cup of Agnes's coffee."

Without thinking, he placed his hand lightly against the small of her back to guide her toward the street. The warmth of her skin through the thin fabric sent an unexpected jolt through him. He pulled his hand back quickly, shoving it into his pocket. That small touch felt oddly intimate, crossing some invisible line he hadn't meant to cross.

If Rachel noticed, she didn't show it. She fell into step beside him, neither saying much in the short walk. At the café, he held the door open for her, the familiar aroma of coffee and home cooking greeting them. Agnes spotted them immediately, bustling over with menus, her eyes twinkling knowingly. "Well, doesn't this feel like a trip back in time? Here for a late dinner?"

"Just coffee and dessert," Jim said.

Agnes directed them to a booth by the window.

"You could be quite the corn hole hustler if you wanted to." Jim resisted the urge to stretch his hand across the table and snatch hold of hers.

Her bright smile flickering slightly, and he saw that shadow again, the one that hinted at the stress she carried beneath the easy laughter. Something was definitely off. Any other woman and he'd believe it was just the stress of her job, but this was Rachel. He might not know the woman she'd become, but he knew enough to know something was seriously bothering her. "So is blueberry pie still your favorite?"

"With lots of whipped cream."

He flashed a smile. "Still like a little pie with your whipped cream?"

"Some things never change."

Again, her smile didn't quite reach her eyes. A frightening thought occurred to him—had he done or said something to upset her? Did placing his hand on her back bother her? Did he tease her too much? What could it have… the deal. She'd seemed rattled when he mentioned it and then she quickly dropped it and went into champion mode. Blast.

"Uh-oh." Rachel's gaze leveled with his. "You're frowning. Don't tell me you actually need the five dollars?"

He tried to laugh, but he couldn't. Instead, thankful there was no one else around them, he leaned forward. "Rachel, if I offended you, I'm really sorry. It wasn't my—"

"Offend me? Of course not. Why would you think that?"

"Back in the park. When I mentioned that deal we'd made. Your mood shifted. It was dumb of me to bring it up. You must think I'm a—"

Cutting him off, she leaned forward, took hold of his hand and squeezed hard. "Hey, you were a good, kind, and special friend. I wasn't offended."

"Then what?" Crud. It was the hand thing.

Her chin dropped for a minute, and she seemed to be contemplating the sins of the world.

"Rachel, once upon a time you trusted me. What's wrong?"

Closing her eyes a long moment, she blew out a sigh and opening her eyes, nodded. "The ranch is in trouble."

And that would explain all the siblings except Kade moving home.

Agnes appeared, setting down two steaming mugs and generous slices of blueberry pie. His plain, hers under a mound of whipped cream. "I figured some things never change." The woman shrugged and hurried away.

"How much trouble?" he asked.

He listened in stunned silence as Rachel explained how their trusted foreman wasn't so trusted. The absurdity of it all hit him harder than he would have expected. This wasn't just a rough patch, this was a crisis, a bizarre, almost unbelievable predicament straight out of a script for a really bad romantic comedy, or maybe a film noir. No wonder she looked stressed.

"It's a miracle that everything worked out so well for my brothers. They're really quite happy. But we can't seem to catch a break when it comes to getting ahead without needing the trust."

His mind was reeling. "How much do you still need?"

Her shoulders deflated. "Too much."

"I'm a good businessman. Maybe I can help, but I need real numbers." When she gave him a figure, he almost fell out of his chair. He made an enviable living but the kind of math the Sweets were playing with was too steep even for him. "And this foreman did that much damage in just over a year?"

"The perfect storm." She sighed. "Dad had borrowed a ton of money against the ranch. If it had been used as intended it would have upped our game, but with Ray in charge, well…" She met his eyes with a vulnerability that made his chest tighten.

"What about the upcoming bank payment that has everyone tearing their hair out? How much is that?"

Her gaze narrowed, and he knew the moment she figured out his game. "I couldn't possibly—"

"Rachel." He cut her off, his tone gentle but firm. "How much?"

She named an amount that made him raise an eyebrow. Substantial, but not impossible. Not for him.

"Let me help." He did his best to lighten the mood with a smile. "I'll trade in all my Italian loafers."

Her lighthearted chuckle was worth the joke.

"For old time's sake?"

Resignation settled over her. "I tell you what, I'll ask the others. See what they think."

"Okay." He nodded. "Fair enough." Now all he had to do was figure out a way to convince the entire Sweet family to let him help.

CHAPTER SEVEN

Maybe it was time for a new bed. That had to be the reason Rachel spent most of the night tossing, turning, and punching her pillow. It couldn't possibly have anything to do with Jim—*Jimmy*—Henderson, his dreamy blue eyes, or the swoon-worthy smile that came with his reminder of their once-upon-a-time marriage deal.

The drive home from the diner had been long and quiet. The fun evening had taken a slightly somber turn when she explained all the challenges they were facing. She could see the muscle in Jim's jaw tightening when she explained all that Ray the crooked foreman had done to them. From leaving the family virtually penniless to her mother being forced to do the work of several men until being thrown by a horse and snarled in barbed wire. Scariest damn day of her life. More so since they'd found their father lifeless, slumped over the kitchen table not much more than a year before her mother's run-in with that fence.

Thank heaven for Brady, he'd been the family hero. She was pretty sure that dog was still getting steak for dinner.

"Yo, you planning on daydreaming or handing me the drill?" Holding the board against the side of the barn, Preston stared at his sister.

"Sorry. Just thinking." She handed him the drill and reached over for another plank. The storm that blew through in the middle of the night had spooked one of their horses so badly he'd kicked the boards right off the barn. Of course, if they'd been able to use the money their father had borrowed to build the new structure they needed, this would never have happened. As of right now, a good deal of this barn was being held together with little more than elbow grease and prayer.

"If it's about how to improve cash flow, I'm listening." Of course he wasn't, the whirring noise of the power drill shoving screws into the aging planks would have drowned her out.

Holding a plank ready to be screwed in, board on board for more strength, her mind wandered back to Jim again. He'd offered to help with the next payment. That would buy them more time, but for what? To find some stranger to bail her out—for a price?

The drill had stopped. Preston pulled the board out of her hand. "Feel free to clue me in on what's got you so spaced out, and if it has anything to do with Jimmy Henderson becoming my new, if temporary, brother-in-law, I'm all ears."

Heat flooded her cheeks. "That's not what I was thinking about." Not exactly. She heaved a deep sigh as she reached for another board. "He offered to lend us the money for the next payment. Buy us some time."

Drill primed to drive another screw into the wall, he stopped and turned to face her. "So, you told him about the problems?"

She nodded.

"Does he know about the trust?"

Again, she bobbed her head.

"But he doesn't want to step in?" Preston bit back a coy grin. "Or does he want benefits like the others?"

Impulse had her smacking her brother on the arm. Hard. "It's not like that."

"Could have fooled me." Preston returned his attention to the work in front of him. "The two of you were mighty close back in the day."

"We were friends."

"That's what you said then." The whir of the drill picked up again.

Friends enough to have made a silly pact about if they reached the whopping old age of thirty, too old to find a soul mate, they'd marry as friends. She didn't know what was more stupid, the idea of marrying because they were friends, or that thirty would be ancient. Of course, she and Jillian had already crossed that threshold without blinking an eye. After all, if sixty is the new forty then she and her sister were still kids.

So why couldn't she get the man, the smile, or the deal, out of her head?

"What brings you to town so early on a Friday morning?" Alice's sister Vicki looked up from a barrel of glitzy corn hole bags.

Setting her purse down on the counter, Alice turned toward her sister. "Ranch needs some more feed. Garret had to go to school, Jillian to the shop, Preston and Rachel are fixing a hole one of the mares kicked in the barn, and Carson is tearing through the tack room looking for Charlie's prize saddle."

"Uh-oh." Liz, her other sister, straightened from where she'd been unpacking a box nearby.

"Yeah. That's what I thought." Alice tried not to think the worst. That saddle was worth a bloody fortune and after all that she'd learned about Ray, she wouldn't put it past him. "But that room is big and messy and I'm hoping it's there somewhere."

Her sister's arm gently rested on hers. "If it's not there, they'll find it somewhere else. There are lots of nooks and crannies on that old place where Charlie might have kept his saddle out of sight from everyone else."

That was exactly what she'd told herself over and over the last few days. Thankful that Carson felt he finally had time to dig a little further.

Straightening her shoulders, she forced a smile. "So, I'm here to get the feed and thought I'd stop and say hi to my two favorite sisters."

"Considering we're your only two sisters, that isn't saying much." Liz loved to tease whenever Alice said something like that and right about now, she appreciated smiling.

"So." Vicki took a step back. "How do you feel about the return of Jimmy Henderson?"

"It's nice to see him again. The kid grew up well."

"You mean filled out well." Liz lifted her chin and flashed a toothy grin. She was in rare form today.

Alice waved her off, then shrugged. "It would be nice to see Rachel and Jillian find good partners."

"Like their brothers," Vicki added.

Liz shook her head. "Maybe we should bottle and sell the local water. Call it a love potion."

The two remaining sisters whipped their head around to stare at the middle sibling.

"You know." She flashed that grin again. "Call it a love potion."

"Love potion?" the two echoed.

Dropping her hands on her hips, Liz sighed. "Well, you have to admit. None of us thought our boys were going to get married before they hit a midlife crisis, and yet here we are, all three of your sons married within a few months of each other."

She and her sisters had always joked that when married men reached the middle of their lives, they'd try to recapture their youths with sports cars or younger women. On the other hand, men who were still single halfway through their life expectancy would want to start a family in order to leave behind a living legacy. Her sons had done that a few years sooner than any of them had thought. At least she'd have to thank her lucky stars that they all found the loves of their lives now and not later. Each son had donated their hefty trust payment to the ranch's debt. She hadn't objected very hard—after all, the Sweet Ranch was part of their legacy.

"You're frowning." Liz inched closer. "What's wrong?"

"Nothing's wrong. Just thinking I'd love to stay and visit longer but I should be getting over to the feed store."

Liz nodded and smiled, apparently appeased with her reasoning. "Will we see you at the game tonight?"

Friday night lights. "Not sure."

"But the alumni game tomorrow?"

All her sons were playing in the annual high school alumni game. The current baseball team would play against the alumni. This was the first year since Charlie died that her sons were going to play. "Definitely wouldn't miss Saturday night."

"Good." Vicki returned her attention to the bin of new bags. "See you then."

Giving them both a quick hug, Alice stepped outside the store, glanced up and down the Main Street that she loved so much, then turned her attention skyward. "I sure do miss you, Charlie, but it's getting easier." She continued to stare at the cloudless Texas sky. "What do you think? Do all these fast-track weddings seem a little coincidental to you? Or are the weddings like sneezes, they always come in three?" Glancing down the street again, she shook her head. "Or is your wife just losing her marbles?"

"What the heck are you doing?" Jim's brother stood over his shoulder, staring at the same screen Jim was.

"Working. What do you think I'm doing?"

Mark shrugged. "I thought you came here to get away from work?"

"I came here to…" why did he come home? "Clear my head."

"And staring at…what the heck is all that?"

"Market fluctuation charts."

"Okay. Staring at whatever clears your head? Cause it strikes me you could have done that in California."

There was no arguing that point, but if he'd learned one thing from his years building a very profitable company, it was that if you snooze you lose. The fact that what he really wanted was to find a way to help Rachel and her family with more than a single bank payment, might have had more to do with his scouring the market today. "If I'd stayed in California, then who would stand over me asking stupid questions?"

His brother smacked him across the back of his head the same way they'd done to each other growing up through the years. They both let out a small snort of laughter. "Seriously, man, what's going on? Are you just taking a mental break, or is staying in Honeysuckle really on the radar?"

Was it? "I honestly don't know."

Mark bobbed his head. "For what it's worth, I haven't seen Mom this happy in a while. She likes having all her chicks in the roost."

"Interesting analogy for a cattle rancher." But he had noticed the same thing. And truth was, he was just as happy to be home as his mother was to have him. He just wasn't sure how much of that had to do with Honeysuckle Texas and how much rested squarely on the shoulders of Rachel Sweet.

"There you are." Wiping her hands on a kitchen towel, his mother entered the room. "Did you make up your mind?"

What was it with everyone? Did they think a man could make life-changing decisions in a heartbeat?

"The game?" His mother obviously misunderstood his blank stare. "Baseball game," she repeated slowly as if he were very hard of hearing or completely daft.

"I forgot to tell him," his brother admitted.

His mom rolled her eyes. "Men. You can't find a snake if it were sitting in front of you and you can't remember to give simple messages." Sporting a quick smile to belie the harshness of her words, she added a quick kiss on Mark's cheek for good measure. "The annual alumni baseball game is tomorrow night. They could use an extra man on the team. Some of the Sweet boys will be playing."

Vaguely, he remembered someone mentioning a game between earlier grads and the current high school baseball team, but he didn't realize it had become an annual event.

"So?" his mom repeated. "I can tell Garret Sweet that you'll play?"

He hadn't held a baseball in so long, he wasn't sure he'd know what to do with it. "As long as it's all in fun, sure, why not?"

CHAPTER EIGHT

"Good grief." Rachel came to a stop just inside the barn doors, her brother nearly knocking into her.

"What the…" Preston glanced at the pile of goods lining the walls and creeping into the walkway. Leading the way, he followed the trail to the tack room and stood to one side so he and Rachel could see inside.

Sitting cross-legged on the floor, papers scattered all about, Carson clutched a few pages in his grip and stared so intently that he hadn't heard them come inside.

"I thought you were looking for a saddle?" Preston asked.

"Found it." Carson waved a thumb over his shoulder, pointing in the general direction of the wall behind him.

Rachel turned to see. Sure enough, their father's saddle leaned into the corner.

"Where was it?" Preston's gaze shifted from the corner to their brother.

"Under a pile of blankets and behind a stack of boxes."

"Boxes?" Preston's brows crinkled to match the surprise Rachel felt. "Why are there boxes in a tack room?"

"Probably because Ray stank at housekeeping. That saddle is worth a fortune, but he probably didn't even know it was there." Carson waved papers in the air as he pushed to his feet. "And under all those blankets, he must have forgotten about these boxes."

"What's in them?" Rachel inched forward to see what Carson referred to.

"All kinds of records. Most useless, but once I found them, I kept digging, hoping to find something that would lead us to Ray or what he sold."

Eyes alight with interest, Preston moved closer, looking over his brother's shoulder. "Find something?"

"Not about Ray." He handed his sister the pages.

Scanning quickly, she shook her head. "This is Clint's work application."

Carson nodded but remained silent.

"And?" She handed it off to Preston at her side.

"Look closely."

Now she scanned it over her brother's shoulder. She and Preston must have found the same thing at the same time, because both their heads snapped up.

"Ex-con?" Preston barely managed to get the words out.

Rachel tugged the papers back and read through more carefully. "For what?"

On a heavy sigh, Carson shook his head slowly. "Yes, and I don't know."

"Crap." Preston raked his fingers through his hair. "Do you think he's in on it?"

"Don't know." Carson shrugged.

"I can't believe it." Rachel stared down at the page. "Have you ever been charged with a crime? Yes. Have you served time in prison? Yes. Are you currently on parole? No." She looked up. "So he served his time?"

"Or escaped," Carson spat out.

"You don't honestly believe that?" Rachel was surprised by her own harsh tone.

Carson shook his head. "No. I don't. He wouldn't be so calm around the sheriff if he were."

"But that doesn't mean he isn't in on it with Ray, or that he's not the one who recently removed the hay baler we found from the shed." Preston retrieved the handwritten application from his sister.

Rachel collapsed on a nearby pile of saddle blankets on top of who knew what. "So what do we do?"

"Fire him," Preston snapped.

"He's been good to Mom, worked hard." Rachel scrubbed her face. "We owe him to at least ask him what's going on."

Carson nodded. "I've run the gamut on fury and confusion, between firing him or beating the truth out of him."

"Conclusion?" Preston leaned against the doorway, the papers still tight in his fist.

"I don't know." Carson reached for the pages. "I see how hard he's worked, how much he clearly worries about Mom, how respectful he is to all the women on this ranch. It isn't adding up."

"So what?" Preston asked. "Tell Mom, see what she thinks?"

Rachel shook her head. "She'll take it hard. Two betrayals, so soon after losing Dad." She didn't have another suggestion, but that one just felt… wrong.

The sound of a vehicle door slamming drew all their attention. Pushing to her feet, Rachel led the way to the open barn doors. The three siblings stood single file as if lining up for a photograph, shortest to the tallest. Though Preston and Carson were nearly the same height, she clearly stood in front to see.

Their mother hopped out of the pickup truck. Her stride steady and strong, a relief after that horrible fall in the barbed wire.

From their left, Clint hopped over the paddock fencing and hurried to where Alice Sweet stood behind the truck, tailgate open, reaching for the large bags of feed. "Hey, let me get that."

"I can do it."

The man nodded. "Yes, ma'am, you can, but that doesn't mean you should."

A smile curled their mother's lips upward as she nodded.

Clint tipped his hat respectfully, and the two exchanged words none of the siblings could hear. There was no telling what was discussed, but their mom nodded again and took a step back as Clint hefted the bag on his shoulder and walked off toward the feed shed.

"Okay." Rachel spun around, staring up at her two brothers. "We do. Not. Tell Mom."

"Agreed," the two men chorused.

"I'll check with the sheriff, see what he knows," Carson added.

"No." Rachel raised her hand. "If the sheriff doesn't know, I don't want to cause Clint trouble."

Preston bobbed his head. "The Farradays. I could call Declan. Dad and Declan's dad were close. He might be able to shed some light on the situation."

All three of them glanced over to where Clint was reaching for another bag.

"For now," Rachel cast a stern gaze in their direction, "let's not stir the pot. We'll keep an eye on him, but this stays between the three of us until... until we're sure what the heck is happening here."

It was pretty obvious to any fool that the idea didn't sit well with the two brothers. She couldn't blame them; she rarely kept anything from her twin, but this was different. This was important. They couldn't let anything else hurt their mother.

Having spent most of his afternoon down a stock market rabbit hole, Jim didn't have any more answers than he'd had when he woke up this morning, after barely sleeping last night. He even wandered outside after breakfast to get some fresh air and hoped that giving his brother a hand mucking out stalls would give him a place to think and gather a better perspective on how to help. What he'd gotten was sore muscles and the need for a long hot shower. After that he'd spent hours on the computer, doing what he'd done every day, practically all day, for years—search for opportunities to make money.

The problem at hand is that the Sweets needed a ton more money than he could make in a few days. Now what he wondered was if Rachel had talked to her siblings about his offer to at least help with a payment or two while they figured out a more long-term solution for the ranch. Though the siblings had come up with an idea, and from what Rachel told him, if all six of them could marry and collect the full trust after a year, the ranch would be free of financial burden and there would even be a little money left to make some of the upgrades their father had originally borrowed money for. Not all, but enough to make their dad proud.

All six. Married. Just for show. The words rattled around his brain like marbles in a pin-ball machine. *Just for show.* Could he do that? Could he stay in Honeysuckle for a year and pretend to be Rachel's husband? Although, it wouldn't be totally pretend. They would indeed be legally hitched, just without any of the benefits afforded by a truly married couple.

"You look like someone stole your favorite candy." His brother slapped him on the shoulder. "Too much hard work for a soft West Coaster?"

Not till his dying day would he admit to his brother that for all his workouts, he was grossly out of shape for ranch work. "Thinking about something Rachel said." He shoved to his feet. "I think I'm going to pop over to the Sweet Ranch. Chat a bit with Garret; see what's the plan for tomorrow night's games."

If his brother had any inkling that Jim had ulterior motives for going to the Sweet ranch, he didn't show it. "Sounds good. And if your baseball skills are as rusty as your stall mucking skills, maybe you can talk them into a little practice game."

"Ha, ha." Jim flashed a toothy grin. "I shouldn't be home late."

Five more minutes and he was out the door. So much on his mind and yet, he was pretty sure there was just one thing at the root of his unease—the deal. A deal that had been meant as fun youthful teasing with a hint of possibility, but an idea that would do more for the Sweets than any market games he could play.

Turning the key in the ignition of the old truck, he put it in gear and drove off. The Sweet ranch wasn't far up the main road from his family. Doc Conroy's property sat between the two ranches. The Sweets had a much larger and older operation than his family, but still, by West Texas standards, a close neighbor. By the time he turned into the Sweet driveway, he'd come to terms with at least one thing—what he was thinking wasn't so much about saving the ranch, but saving Rachel from another man. Or maybe, saving himself.

As soon as he came to a stop in front of the large home, Brady and another dog came trotting over to the truck, a little boy who had to be Mason jogged behind them. Carefully, Jim opened his door and eased out of the vehicle. Neither dog looked terribly angry, and yet, neither budged from Mason's side. His first step forward and Brady lifted a lip, exposing one very long and sharp tooth. The other dog did the same, and bless that little boy's heart, he latched an arm around each dog's neck and simply announced to them, "He's a friend."

Instantly the dog's hackles eased, and the semi snarl faded, but Jim cut a wide berth around the boy, nonetheless. There wasn't the slightest doubt in his mind that if he made a single wrong move, those dogs would protect that child with their lives—and he had no intention of proving his suspicions.

"Well, what a nice surprise." Alice Sweet appeared on the porch. In a button-down shirt with jeans and boots and a buckle to remind him that once upon a time the woman had been a barrel racing champ, she looked every bit the image of the rancher's wife... widow.

"Hope I'm not intruding."

"Now James Henderson, have you been gone so long that you've forgotten what it means to be neighborly?"

Swallowing a chuckle, he resisted the urge to dig his booted toe into the dirt. "No, ma'am."

"Then come on in and I'll get you a drink."

"Thank you." He followed her onto the porch and into the house. His gaze darted around. Little had changed through the years except things were a lot quieter. "I was hoping to have a chat with your sons."

"Oh?" Her brows lifted slightly.

"About the game tomorrow."

"Oh." A smile touched her lips. "They're in their dad's office. I swear, the last few months those kids gather in that room so often I'm starting to think they're digging under the floorboards for gold."

Now was a good time for him to laugh in earnest. Especially since he knew why the siblings gathered so often.

"You know how to find them. Go on." Alice smiled, nodded, and politely shooed him toward the office. Tapping on the door jam with his college ring, he waited till everyone looked up before stepping into the room. "Your mom tells me y'all are digging for gold."

Jillian chuckled. "I wish."

"Jim?" Rachel popped up from her seat.

He tried to contain the smile that threatened to take over his face at the mere sight of her. "Have you had a chance to discuss my offer yet?"

"She was just telling us." Preston looked up from the desk.

Jillian shook her head. "We need another loan like we need a hole in our heads."

"I understand," he nodded, "but this would be different. Interest rates aren't great right now anyhow, so an interest-free loan with no payments until you can get back on your feet would help."

Eyes darted back and forth. Carson looked at Garret, Garret looked at Preston, Jillian looked to Jim and eventually, all eyes landed on Rachel.

"Why is everyone looking at me?"

Carson hefted a shoulder. "It's tempting, but you're not on board?"

She shook her head, her gaze drifting toward him. "Best way I know to kill a friendship is to borrow money."

"Don't you plan to pay it back?" he teased, or at least hoped that's how it sounded to his audience.

"Of course we do." Her voice rose an octave with indignation.

"See?" He flashed a smile and faced the others. "Then

what's the problem?"

Rachel collapsed again in the chair. "Besides it's just a temporary fix, like shoving chewing gum into the hole in the dike. It just feels wrong."

"She's right," Jillian chimed in. "We can't take advantage of your friendship."

"Why not?" Preston stared at his sister. "We let Sarah marry me. No one was worried about a family friendship then."

Jillian's head snapped over to her sister and Rachel leveled her gaze with her sister's for a long moment before finally shaking her head with a shrug.

"Excuse me." Jim cleared his throat. "I wasn't finished."

All eyes turned to him, and he took a deep breath.

He might very well have lost his mind, but here went nothing. "What if I step in and play happily ever after the same way the rest of you have?"

CHAPTER NINE

Jim's words hung in the air, almost visible in their impact. Not what anyone had expected, her siblings remained silent, everyone processing the implications of the man's announcement. Preston's mouth opened and closed once then twice before he wordlessly dropped back into their father's chair.

"Could you please clarify what you mean?" Jillian finally broke the stunned quiet.

"Marry Rachel." Jim's voice didn't waver. "For the trust. Just like the others did."

Except only one marriage was for the trust, by the time the other two married, it had been for love. "You can't do that. You're going back to California."

Carson glanced at Garret, who in turn looked at Preston. The three brothers seemed to be having some silent conversation that excluded everyone else in the room.

"That's not a given. Besides, lots of people have commuter relationships." Jim inched closer to where Rachel sat.

"Halfway across the country?" She shook her head. "Who would believe that?"

"Lots of people." Jillian quickly clamped her mouth shut and heaved an apologetic shrug at Rachel's pointed glare. "Sorry, just saying, actors do it all the time. Live on one coast and commute to the other."

"We're not actors," she snapped back.

Preston tipped his head to one side and shrugged. "So does Corporate America. One partner works overseas and the other stays home and gets the kids to school on time."

"There are no kids." Again, Rachel responded quickly.

Her mind scrambling. Were all her siblings in agreement with Jim? Didn't they see the problems a fake marriage with this guy, a man who could too easily work his way back into her heart, would pose?

"Why are you so opposed?" His gaze narrowed, his focus entirely on her. "Your brothers all did it. Sarah, Jackie, Jessica—they all agreed to help. Why am I any different?"

How could she possibly answer that when she couldn't even think straight?

Carson cleared his throat. "So, you're proposing commuting to California?"

"I have partners who are perfectly capable of running things. Remote work is a thing these days. I can make it work." Jim shrugged as if relocating his entire life was no more complicated than deciding what to have for dinner.

"For a year?" Jillian's tone suggested she didn't believe him.

Jim sucked in a shallow breath and slowly nodded. "If that's what it takes."

Rachel's pulse pounded in her ears. She couldn't process this. Jim—her childhood friend, the boy who'd skipped rocks with her, the teenager who'd taught her to drive a stick shift, the man who'd just walked back into her life days ago, who they'd once made a pseudo-marriage pact for real—was offering to marry her for pretend. How the hell was she supposed to deal with that?

"For the trust payment to kick in," Garret set his glass on the end table, "you'd have to stay married the full year. We'd still get a boost up front, but we'd need you to put up with our sister for a whole year to get the final payoff."

"Hey," Rachel burst out, "what do you mean put up with me? I'd have to put up with him!" For some reason she couldn't possibly understand, her words made Jim smile, her brothers quickly following suit.

Calmly, still smiling, Jim nodded. "I understand the terms."

"No benefits," Jillian added pointedly.

"Jill." Rachel felt her cheeks flame.

"What?" Her twin raised an eyebrow. "Everyone's thinking it. If Jim's going to agree to this, he needs to understand all the rules."

"I do," Jim confirmed, his expression unchanged.

Preston leaned forward, elbows on the desk. "Why would you do this?"

Jim's eyes found hers again. "Because Rachel would do the same for me if our situations were reversed."

The simple truth of it struck her silent. He was right. If his family had been in trouble, if there had been anything she could do to help, she would have. Without hesitation. So why was this so hard? It should be a no-brainer. They needed money. She'd been looking for someone to do just what Jim was offering. Willing to make an arrangement with a total stranger. Yet, she couldn't bring herself to say yes to Jim.

Clearly, this decision was ultimately hers. And everyone in the room knew it, as all eyes were on her, waiting for her response.

"I…" Rachel swallowed hard. "I need to think."

As if that was a perfectly reasonable response to a marriage proposal, even a fake one, Jim nodded. "Of course."

"Since we're not settling anything tonight," Preston pushed to his feet, "my wife is expecting me to take her to the football game."

"Right." Carson stood as well. "If we win tonight, we're in the playoffs."

"Shall we go?" Jim's gaze settled on hers. "Might be fun?"

Anything she did with Jim was always fun. She supposed that might be part of the problem. Adjusting to not having Jim around after college had been tough. At first, really tough. How would she handle losing him again after a year of house play? Maybe he was right. A night away from the ranch and the financial problems and rooting for their high school team was exactly what she needed.

"Okay." She nodded. "Let me grab a jacket. It's getting chillier most nights."

Jim chuckled. "Don't sound so excited. I promise you won't have to put up with too much tonight."

"Ha ha," she teased back. Surprised to discover, despite all her concerns, she was actually looking forward to watching the game with him. Lord, talk about a woman's prerogative to change her mind. She'd better find hers and soon.

Outside, holding open the passenger door, as Rachel climbed into Jim's truck, their eyes met briefly. The intensity in her gaze—the fear in her eyes—clutched at his heart. Was it fear of the situation, the consequences or heaven forbid, him?

Once he'd settled behind the wheel, he started the engine and glanced in her direction. "You don't have to say yes. I'll help with payments as much as I can until you guys get out of this."

"I know." She fastened her seatbelt.

Lord help him, the next part was hard to say, "Or until you find someone more suitable."

Her eyes flew open, and her head snapped around. "More suitable?"

"Someone you feel comfortable saying yes to." Turning onto the road, he eased his grip on the steering wheel.

"There isn't anyone I would ever feel more comfortable with." Her gaze drifted away from him and out the windshield. "That's the problem."

"I'm sorry, what?" Understanding women wasn't always his best strength, but right about now, he was horribly confused.

She heaved a deep sigh and loosening her safety belt, turned her whole body to face him. "I can't think of anyone who knew me better than you did. Anyone who I felt more at home with. Or anyone I would have ever made a marriage pact with—even in jest."

"I don't understand. So, what's the problem?"

Her lower lip seemed to quiver ever so slightly, before she lifted her chin and blinking once, leveled her gaze with his. "I guess, the long and short of it is, if this crazy idea goes south, then I'd lose you forever." Holding her hand up, she shifted again. "It's one thing knowing you're living happily in California and if I were so inclined I could grab my phone, call you, and you'd be happy to hear from me. It's a whole different story knowing that my calls will never again be welcome."

"First of all," his grip on the wheel tightened again, "I wasn't living happily in California, and secondly, nothing that happens in the next year could possibly ruin our friendship. Hell," he dared glance in her direction, "it's only because we're such good friends, can talk about anything, anytime, that I'm even considering this crazy idea."

"So you agree it's crazy?" To his surprise, her mood seemed to shift, and a smile threatened to appear.

"Of course I do, but this isn't a childhood blood brother pack where we spit in our palms and shake. This is to save the Sweet Ranch and everything your family holds dear."

Turning around to face forward, Rachel's gaze fixed on something in the distance. "If you promise me that we'll always be friends, then yes, we can do this."

When she turned away from him, he'd braced himself for an absolute, positive, and not a chance in hell resounding no. Instead, he felt an odd urge to do a fist pump and howl at the moon as if this were a real proposal and a forever after response. Stilling his surging enthusiasm, he curtailed his smile and looked to her. "Sounds like we have a new deal. So." Turning away, he refocused on the road. "Let's get to town and cheer our team on."

To his delight, a bright smile bloomed. "Go Hawks!"

On the edge of town, Jim pulled the truck into a spot near the high school stadium, the roar of the crowd already audible over the engine's idle. Friday night lights. The sounds, the smells—popcorn, grilled burgers, cut grass— were instantly familiar, transporting him back years. It felt strangely good. Especially with Rachel beside him, a tentative excitement now replacing the worry in her eyes.

"Smells amazing." Rachel sniffed the air as they walked towards the entrance gate, her shoulder brushing his companionably. "Popcorn is definitely required."

"Absolutely." Jim grinned, feeling way more at ease than he probably should be for a man who had just agreed to a marital business arrangement.

They navigated the crowded entrance, paid their admission, and immediately headed for the concession stand. Loaded up with a giant tub of popcorn and two sodas, they found seats midway up the bleachers on the home side, settling in just as the Hawks scored their first touchdown.

The crowd erupted. Without thinking, Jim high-fived Rachel, the shared moment of hometown pride feeling completely natural. The game was a nail-biter, the score seesawing back and forth. They cheered, groaned, and offered unsolicited advice to the referees along with the rest of the Honeysuckle faithful. Jim found himself easily falling back into their old rhythm—playful jabs, shared glances, finishing each other's sentences about a botched play or a brilliant tackle.

The bleachers vibrated with stomping feet as the crowd roared. Fourth quarter, tied game, and the Hawks' quarterback had just dodged three defenders to scramble for a crucial first down. Jim found himself on his feet alongside everyone else, his voice joining the collective cheer.

"Did you see that move?" Rachel bounced excitedly beside him. "Reminds me of Garret back in the day."

"Kid's got talent," Jim agreed, settling back onto the metal bench. Their shoulders bumped, and neither moved away.

Her gaze riveted on the field, Rachel nodded. "We might actually make it all the way to state this year."

"Popcorn?" Jim held out the nearly empty tub they'd been sharing.

Rachel reached in just as the running back broke free, streaking down the sideline. In the excitement, Jim's arm jerked up, sending popcorn flying. Most of it landed in Rachel's hair, a few kernels sliding down the front of her jacket.

"Sorry," he managed between laughs.

"Smooth, Henderson." Rachel plucked a piece from her collar and popped it in her mouth. "Very smooth."

Their eyes met, and suddenly they were both laughing like teenagers again—the kind of deep, genuine laughter that made your sides hurt. The kind they used to share before life got complicated.

"Touchdown!" The announcer's voice boomed through the speakers, and once again the stands erupted.

Rachel grabbed his arm. "We're ahead with only two minutes left."

The next plays unfolded in a blur of tension and noise. The visiting team drove desperately downfield, gaining yards in chunks that made the home crowd groan. With thirty seconds left, they were in field goal range—a tie game again if they made it.

"I can't watch." Rachel buried her face in Jim's shoulder.

The snap. The hold. The kick sailing toward the uprights—and then veering wide left at the last possible second.

The stadium exploded. Rachel launched herself up with a scream of joy, throwing her arms around Jim's neck. He caught her without thinking, lifting her slightly off her feet in the excitement of the moment.

"We won!" she shouted above the noise, her face inches from his.

Time seemed to slow. Her eyes, bright with victory and something else—something warmer—held his. For a heartbeat, maybe two, the celebrating crowd around them faded to background noise.

"That we did, Mrs. Henderson."

Her eyes widened, she slid back down, her hands moving to rest against his chest.

"Just trying it on for size," he reassured before taking a step back. The last thing he wanted to do was set her ill at ease again.

A twinkle reached her eyes, and a smile settled in place. "That we did, Mr. Henderson. That we did."

CHAPTER TEN

Finished with her morning chores, Rachel stretched her tired muscles. The rhythm of ranch life was a familiar comfort despite the underlying uncertainty churning within her. Thoughts of soon marrying Jim Henderson sporadically sent flutters of panic tempered with something else she didn't quite understand straight through her. From the top of her head to the tip of her toes, every nerve ending was on high alert.

What she needed to cut the edge was a good warm cup of coffee. She rounded the corner of the barn, heading toward the house, when the rumble of a large engine caught her attention. A sizable truck made its way up the long drive, kicking up dust in its wake.

"What in the world?" she murmured, changing course to intercept the unexpected visitor. As she approached the front of the house, she spotted her mother standing on the porch, practically bouncing on her toes. Alice Sweet was many things, but a bouncer wasn't usually one of them.

One by one, her brothers and their wives appeared. Garret and Preston coming around from the other side of the house, Carson and her sisters-in-law from inside. By the time the driver had hopped out of the cab of the truck, everyone home had gathered round, her mother's eyes alight with mischief.

"Were you expecting a delivery?" Carson addressed his mother, his gaze on the driver circling the truck.

"I am."

The driver approached the group, clipboard in hand, and scanned left to right. "Do you want this in the house?"

"No." Their mom shook her head, her gaze darting off

into the distance just as Clint drove up the old dirt road that led past the barns to the rest of Sweet family land.

"Sorry I'm late." Clint nodded at their mother.

"No problem." She smiled then turned to the driver. "Let's get a look at what's inside then Clint here will take you to where we'll unload."

The driver hit a lever, and the rear rose up and the tail gate lowered. Handing her the clipboard, he said, "You'll see it's all here."

Taking minced steps, Jackie approached the truck. "Is that…?" Her hands flew to her mouth. "That's my great-grandmother's bedroom set."

Their mom's head nodded so quickly, Rachel was surprised it didn't snap off. "Your grandmother mentioned at the wedding that she had several pieces she thought you'd enjoy. To remind you of home. Of happy days."

Jackie nodded. "I used to sit at the vanity and play famous actress. Grams said it suited me."

Already back in his truck, his arm out the window, Clint motioned for the driver to follow.

"Where's he going?" Preston asked.

"There's no room for the furniture here," the family matriarch said with a smile. "Hop into the Suburban and I'll show you."

The siblings looked from one to the other, no one moving.

"All of you," their mom called from the driver's side. "And get the lead out."

Suddenly scrambling like ants after their mound had been kicked over, everyone climbed into the vehicle. Rachel almost didn't get the door closed behind her before her mom hit the gas.

At her side, Sarah leaned over and softly whispered, "Do you know what's going on?"

Rachel shook her head. It wasn't like her mom to be so secretive, but then again, nothing around the Sweet ranch was like it used to be.

The short drive took them about a mile from the main house. Clint and the delivery truck were stopped ahead past a low rising crop of mesquite trees. As their mom drove around the truck, a small blue cottage with white trim came into view.

"What the…" Carson was the first to mutter what the others were thinking.

It took Rachel a few long moments to register that the cute cottage equipped with a bright red door, black shutters, and flowers in the window boxes, was in exactly the same spot as the ancient foreman's cabin. A cabin that had fallen into such disrepair, the family had stopped using it for storage over a decade ago.

"I don't understand," someone muttered.

"That makes two of us," another voice agreed.

"Let's go inside." Not waiting for a response, their mother trotted to the front door, cutting off the driver and his associate, carrying the first piece into the house. "Straight ahead, gentlemen."

With a nod, the two guys carrying a dresser strode up the two steps, into the house, and continued straight as directed.

Rachel couldn't believe her eyes. They stood in the middle of a good-sized parlor with an old-fashioned stone fireplace. To their left, a small but efficient kitchen with white cabinets and butcher block counters. A table with two chairs was tucked into a cove off the kitchen.

Mouths slightly ajar, the family dispersed, one person looking out the living room window, another running their hand over the countertops, Jackie hurried down the hall after her ancestor's furniture.

"How?" Carson asked no one in particular.

"I know you and Jess were married before Garret and Jackie, but this place just wouldn't have been big enough for the three of you, but it's perfect for two."

Garret's head whipped around. "This is for us?"

Again, their mom nodded enthusiastically.

"But how?" Carson repeated.

Clint came in with an old marble topped walnut washstand. "Where do you want this?"

Their mom looked to Jackie who had come from the

bedroom, her eyes dewy with moisture. "I, I don't know."

"Why don't you set it in the bath, maybe they can use it to store towels."

With a nod, Clint continued down the short hall.

"Mom," Carson said more forcefully.

"Yes. I know. How. It was really quite easy. I'd been talking with Jackie's grandmother, and she knows that the ranch is going through a rough patch."

Rachel had to bite her tongue not to point out what an understatement that was.

"But she had some money set aside for Jackie's wedding that wasn't needed so we agreed, if she could pay for materials, we would supply the labor."

"We?" Sarah asked.

"Well, Clint did most of it. I helped where I could."

"Don't let her sell herself short." Clint emerged from the hall bath. "This woman can wield a hammer and sander with the best of them."

"It took longer than I'd thought, but at least we got it done before the truck arrived." Alice Sweet turned to Clint. "What we discussed yesterday?"

"Right." He nodded. "I piled the wedding gifts out of the way against the far wall in the bedroom."

"Thank you," Mom smiled. "I considered unpacking for you, but then thought better of it. Deciding where to put everything in your first home is most of the fun. Also, Aunt Vicki says if you want to use the old leather sofa from her game room until you shop for your own, it's all yours. No one uses that room or sofa much since the boys moved away."

"Tell Aunt Vicki we said thank you." Jackie looked up at her husband, her smile so bright the woman could have lit the way for most of West Texas.

The ding of an incoming message sounded. Rachel would have ignored it if it hadn't been followed by another ding and then another, almost on top of each other. Glancing down at her phone, she read the first message. From Jillian. *Cat's out of the bag. Though they are putting the cart before the horse. Bless every bleached blonde strand on Iris Hathaways head.*

Reviewing emails, putting out a few embers before they became problematic fires, relishing in delegating major responsibility to his partners, Jim sipped his coffee at his parents' kitchen table. His mother had gone to town for her weekly hair appointment, his father and brother were out checking fence lines, and the remodeling crew didn't work weekends, leaving him with a rare moment of peaceful solitude to contemplate his future. His future with Rachel.

The word "wife" kept circling in his mind, attaching itself to her name despite his attempts to maintain some perspective. This was a business arrangement, he reminded himself. A mutual solution to a problem. Nothing more. Interrupting his thoughts, his cell phone vibrated against the table, Rachel's name lighting up the screen.

We need to talk... in person. Can you come over?

The undertone of urgency in her text sent a jolt of concern through him.

Just getting coffee, can come right now.

Her reply came immediately: *Perfect. Meet me at the house.*

His hair still damp from a shower and his coffee left sitting on the kitchen table, Jim pulled into the ranch driveway. The truck had barely rolled to a stop when Rachel came scurrying down the porch steps. His gut did a somersault; nothing good could come from the look on her face.

Slamming the car door behind him, he met her halfway to the house. "What's going on?"

Rachel heaved in a deep breath and blew it out softly. "Apparently, we're married."

"We're... what?"

"Sorry. They think we're married." Looking over his shoulder, she reached for his hand and tugged. "Let's do this inside."

Seated in the front room with most of her siblings, Rachel rambled on so quickly, he was only able to process every other word. The gist being after playfully calling her Mrs. Henderson at last night's game, the gossip mill went to work.

The front door burst open and Jillian, the only missing sibling, rushed in, slightly out of breath. "Got someone to cover the shop." She dropped her purse on the side table. "You two no longer have time to think this through. The whole town is buzzing and once Mom checks her phone, the circus will begin in earnest. This is either a gift from heaven or hell, and damned if I know which."

"Wait, where is your mother?" Jim asked.

"She and Clint stayed behind with Garret and Jackie to help unload furniture," Carson explained. "The rest of us headed back here when Rachel got the first text from Jillian."

Jim blinked. "Do I want to know what furniture and where?"

"I'll tell you later." Rachel squeezed his hand. "We have to come up with a plan of how to proceed."

"Okay. Let me see if I understand correctly. Someone overheard me call Rachel Mrs. Henderson at the game last night, and now the whole town thinks we secretly got married?"

Jillian nodded vigorously. "If there's one person in Honeysuckle who can spread news faster than wildfire, it's Iris Hathaway."

"But she didn't start it," Preston added. "According to what I've pieced together, Mrs. Miller was the one who overheard you at the game and mentioned it this morning to Dot Wilkins at the pharmacy when Mrs. Miller picked up her blood pressure medication."

"Then over coffee, Dot told Agnes at the café," Carson continued, "where Iris Hathaway was having breakfast with half the Garden Club."

"And once Iris knew…" Rachel threw up her hands.

"Exactly," Jillian confirmed. "Iris rushed straight to Corn Hole Heaven to tell our aunts, then to the Bluebonnet Inn where the Ladies' Auxiliary was setting up for next week's fundraiser, and by noon today, I guarantee there won't be a soul in the county who doesn't think you two are hitched."

Jillian was absolutely right. Whether or not this unexpected rumor was a blessing or a curse, he didn't have a clue.

CHAPTER ELEVEN

The controlled chaos in the study was almost comical if the stakes weren't so damn high. Jim watched Rachel try to field Jillian's rapid-fire suggestions while Preston and Carson looked ready to strategize a corporate takeover of the Honeysuckle rumor mill. They were panicking, and honestly, he couldn't blame them. The gossip wasn't just inconvenient; it forced their hand, demanding immediate action and a believable performance.

"Okay," his voice cut through the noise with quiet authority. "Clearly, we can't control the gossip right now. Freaking out won't help." He looked directly at Rachel, holding her gaze. "Rach, can we talk? Outside? Just for a minute?"

She nodded, seemingly grateful for the lifeline. Jim placed his hand gently at the small of her back, guiding her through the house onto the back porch. The crisp morning air was a welcome relief from the tension inside.

Once the door closed behind them, he guided her towards the old wooden swing, waiting until she sat before taking the spot beside her. The chains creaked softly as it swayed.

"This is crazy, Jim. The whole town thinks we're already married."

"I know." He took her hand in his. The gesture felt both strange and completely natural. "But maybe this isn't entirely bad."

"I'm not sure it's entirely good, either. We haven't talked through any of the details. When do we tell our families, when do we marry, and where. Then there's the living arrangements. There are no apartments to be had right now, and even if there were, all my funds are going toward the ranch, not rent." Her arms flew up and then dropped heavily in her lap. "Maybe we should go with the flow, say that we are indeed married, and then sneak off to Oklahoma for a few hours."

He had to bite back a smile. She was so upset, and her nose was doing that crinkly thing again making him want ever so badly to smile at her. "Breathe," he whispered, reaching again for her hand and gently squeezed. "We can't lie about already being married. The bank will see the actual date on the certificate, and that could complicate the trust payment."

"Right," she sighed, but didn't pull her hand away.

"I have money, but if there aren't any apartments then it's a moot point. And we certainly can't stay with my parents on the sofa bed. I still need to pop back to California on occasion, but the rest of the time, we're probably going to have to do like your brothers and stay here."

"Here?" The way her eyes rolled upward, and a low growl rumbled in her throat, he got the feeling he was missing something. "I have a full bed. Carson's old room has a queen."

He nodded. Not till this moment did he realize how close he would have to actually be—all night—if they went through with this.

"Maybe I can talk Carson and Jess into going back to his room so we can have the master. King-size bed will make sharing way easier. I'm a tosser."

"Tosser?"

"I tend to flip and toss when I sleep."

Flip and toss. While she sleeps. Oh, those were some images he didn't need to be dwelling on. "As far as when to tell our parents, I don't think we've been left a choice. If we deny all the rumors, it will only set your plans back and there isn't time for that. So, we embrace the rumors." He leaned closer instinctively, wanting to reassure her, wanting to bridge the slight distance that felt wrong between them now. "What if we share the sort of truth?"

Her nose crinkled again.

"We tell them I came home looking for something real." He held her gaze, letting the honesty of that part sink in. "And I found it when I ran into you. We reconnected, things clicked fast, maybe faster than we planned thanks to..." he gestured vaguely, "circumstances. We decided life's too short to wait."

"So, you're calling me Mrs. Henderson was just seeing how it rolled off your tongue?"

Now he did smile at her repeating what he'd said last night. "See? Sort of the truth."

She nodded, the slightest hint of a smile teasing one corner of her mouth. "We can tell them we're going to the courthouse for a license and getting married in three days."

Three days. He tried not to tense. Moving up the timeline because the cat was out of the proverbial bag made sense, but three days? "Three days."

She swallowed, hard, her throat working. He reached up, his thumb brushing a stray wisp of hair from her cheek, the silky texture sending an unexpected jolt through him. "We're going to have to get comfortable with this," he murmured, his voice dropping lower. "Touching. Showing affection. Looking natural. Selling it." His hand cupped her jaw gently, needing her to believe him, needing her to be okay with this. "Think you can do that? Handle the questions, the gossip, Mom probably planning a reception already?"

She searched his eyes for a long moment, then leaned almost imperceptibly into his touch. A tiny spark of something—trust? Hope?—flickered in her gaze. "Yes," she whispered, the sound barely audible but carrying immense weight. "If you're really in this, Jim. If you promise... friends, always?"

Relief, potent and unexpected, washed through him. "I'm in, Rach," his voice husky and raw. "All in. And friends, always. Promise." He wanted to kiss her then, seal the promise, blur the lines completely. But just as he leaned fractionally closer, the back door creaked open.

Alice Sweet stood frozen in the doorway, her eyes wide as she took in the sight of her daughter in Jim's arms. "So it's true," she said softly.

Rachel tensed against him, but Jim kept his arm firmly around her waist.

"Mom," Rachel drew from Jim's support, "we need to talk."

The energy crackling under the Saturday night stadium lights was infectious. Rachel found herself squeezed onto the slightly-too-narrow bleacher bench between Alice and Jillian, with Sarah Sue, Jess, and Jackie filling out the row. Down on the field, the alumni team—including Preston, Carson, Garret, and Jim—were warming up, their easy laughter and familiar banter carrying up to the stands. Seeing Jim out there in a Hawks baseball jersey and cap, looking completely at ease bantering with her brothers, seemed so surreal and yet so familiar.

Since their intense porch conversation, their hasty agreement, and her mother's easy acceptance of their explanation for all the confusion, an unexpected calm had settled over her. Now, surrounded by the cheerful chaos of the game, she tamped down a rising sense of panic, steeled her spine, and focused on the field. *Showtime.*

The game started, a match between Honeysuckle past and present. Rachel found herself cheering, genuinely caught up in the simple fun of it all. Every time Jim came up to bat or made a play at third base, her focus narrowed, her applause a little louder, her breath catching just slightly. She registered the happy sighs from Alice, the enthusiastic waves from Aunts Vicki and Liz a few rows down. The whole town was watching them, weaving the narrative the gossip mill had started. She just had to play her part.

After a couple of innings, Rachel made her way to the fence, deliberately carrying water bottles. When Jim jogged over, she handed him one with a smile meant for their audience.

"Thirsty?" she asked, letting her fingers brush his as she

passed the bottle through a break in the fence.

"Very," he replied, his voice dropping to a low pitch that made her pulse quicken. He took a long drink, then deliberately reached through the chain links to tuck a strand of hair behind her ear. The gesture was tender, intimate—perfectly calculated for the onlookers. Later, when he slid into third, she pretended concern, brushing dirt from his uniform through the fence.

Throughout the next two innings, they continued their performance. Back in the stands, Rachel cheered extra loudly when Jim made a play. He blew her a kiss after a base hit. Each touch, each look, was a deliberate piece of their charade.

Top of the sixth inning, alumni were leading by a couple of runs. Jim was at the plate, focused, determined. He'd already gotten a solid single earlier. The high school pitcher, a lanky kid with more ambition than control, wound up. The pitch came in fast, way inside. Too inside.

Jim twisted, jerking away, but not far enough. The baseball slammed into his ribs, just below his arm. Clutching his side, his face contorted in agony; he didn't just stumble, he collapsed, hitting the dirt hard.

Everything stopped. The crowd noise died instantly to a horrified hush. Rachel's heart leaped into her throat, icy fear washing over her in a crippling wave. She shot to her feet. Practically leap frogging over her mother's knees, she bolted down the steps and through the dugout gate onto the field. Jim, her only focus, still down on the dirt, now surrounded by her brothers.

"Let me through!" She pushed past Garret, dropping to her knees beside Jim just as Preston helped him sit up. Dust clouded around them. Jim's face was tight, pale under the stadium lights, his breath coming in shallow gasps as he clutched his side.

"Jim," she grabbed his free hand, "talk to me. Where does it hurt most? Can you breathe okay?" Her social worker instincts kicked in, overriding the panic, demanding assessment.

He squeezed her hand weakly, managing a grimace that

was probably meant to be reassuring. "Ribs... took the hit. Knocked... wind out..." Each word seemed an effort.

"Okay, okay." She kept her voice calm, even though her heart was hammering against her own ribs. She ran her eyes quickly over him, looking for any other obvious injury. "Don't try to talk too much. Just breathe slow."

Doc Conroy jogged over, kneeling on Jim's other side. "Let's take a look, Jim."

Rachel reluctantly released Jim's hand to give the doctor space but stayed kneeling close, her eyes locked on Jim's face, searching for any flicker of worsening pain. Preston and Carson hovered nearby, their usual teasing banter replaced with tense silence. Garret stood just behind Rachel, a grounding presence. A literal picture of her reality, her brothers always had her back.

Doc gently probed the area.

Jim hissed in pain, closing his eyes briefly. "That hurts like hell," he muttered through gritted teeth.

"Probably cracked a rib or two. Safe to say you're not finishing the game." The doc's effort at humor helped take the edge off the fear that had gripped her and wouldn't let go.

"Can you stand?" Preston asked Jim gently.

Jim nodded.

Instinctively, Rachel moved to help, getting her shoulder under his good arm as Preston took the other side. Garret provided support from behind. Slowly, carefully, they helped Jim to his feet. He swayed slightly, his weight heavy against her, his breathing still tight.

"Easy does it," she murmured, automatically adjusting her steps to match his slow, pained shuffle towards the dugout. The still quiet crowd began applauding as he carefully made his way off the field.

They reached the dugout, easing Jim carefully onto the bench. Doc eyed him carefully. "We need to get you to the hospital. Make sure you didn't bruise anything internally."

She could read Jim's face, even in pain. As he opened his mouth, she knew he was going to say no, that he was fine. Instead, she squeezed his hand. "I can bring the

Suburban onto the field."

Doc nodded. "That'll work. But take it slow. Every notch in the road is going to feel like a crater."

Nodding, she gave him a kiss on the forehead. "I'll be right back."

A shaky smile briefly touched his lips. "That was worth taking the hit for."

If he hadn't already been in pain, she would have smacked him. Instead, she merely shook her head then turned and rushed to her car, her sister catching up with her.

"That was a great performance." Jillian fell in step beside her. "If anybody didn't believe you two were an item before, they certainly will now."

Performance? Is that what her sister thought? She'd been scared to death, not just that Jim was hurt, but that she might lose him. And wasn't that one hell of a revelation.

CHAPTER TWELVE

Rachel had no idea why she bothered to climb into bed last night. The hospital confirmed Jim had no broken or even cracked ribs, only bruised. Which, as far as Jim was concerned, hurt just the same. Apparently, his reflexes were better than she'd thought. He'd twisted just enough for the baseball to graze his side, not slam into it. Though from what was explained to her, a baseball pitched at eighty miles an hour is going to hurt when it skips over a man's rib cage like stones on water. The news should have been great, wonderful, a relief. For the most part, the news of no breaks was great, but that didn't help her get some sleep. Regardless of what the doctor had explained, she was still worried about him.

After his release, she'd driven him home and Garret followed in Jim's truck. Somehow the grapevine had failed to reach his mother—probably a good thing. Everyone had fawned over him and finally, he was settled with the meds kicking in, and Rachel and Garret headed home.

"I don't understand what the hurry is." Her mother slapped bread across the counter as if it had somehow offended her. Putting together the fixings for double grilled cheese sandwiches to go with her homemade tomato soup, she shook her head. "What is it with all of you and weddings? Anyone would think you were allergic to them."

"Not all weddings, just big ones." As a little girl, she had dreamed of a big fancy wedding with a long train, lots of bridesmaids, and, of course, flowers. The older she got, the more all those ideas seemed to be nothing but a waste of money. Now that they were in such dire straits, there was nothing about a fancy dress, a ton of food, and the whole town watching that appealed.

Her mother peeled slices of cheese out of the packets. "Fine. A small wedding. But that doesn't explain, what's the hurry?"

It took Rachel a few moments to shuffle through answers that might work, when a light bulb went off. "When did you know you wanted to marry Dad?"

A huge smile bloomed and her previously rough movements slowed. "At the Harvest dance when he asked me to dance and told me he liked the new way I'd done my hair." She blew out a little sigh. "Men never noticed things like that, but your dad, he noticed and remembered everything."

She nodded. "And how long had you been dating?"

"Oh," her mom shook her head and reached for the Swiss cheese, "that was the first time he got up the nerve to ask me out."

Rachel just stood, silently, waiting for her mother to connect the dots.

Her mom waved a finger at her. "You're sneaky, you know."

"I've got a lot of practice. In my line of work, the trick to getting people to talk is to ask the right questions. You learn more, accomplish more when you let folks tell their story."

"Never ask a yes or no question." Her mom smiled. "You've said that before."

"Right. If I ask, are you okay, I'll get a yes or no answer. On the other hand, if I say, tell me how you're feeling, we might get somewhere." Now it was her turn to smile. "And nice to know you listened."

"To every word." Turning, her mom went back to assembling sandwiches. "Any news on how Jim is doing this morning?"

"No. I called, but his mom said he was sleeping, and she didn't want to disturb him."

"Smart woman. Rest is important when you're healing."

She knew that, but she still wanted to see for herself. Glancing up at the wall clock, she debated how annoyed would his mom be if she just showed up at the Henderson home? Before she could steal up the courage to drive over, the front door squeaked open, and she made a mental note to oil the hinges.

"Look who I found shuffling outside." Garret came in the front door, hung his hat on a nearby hook, and stood waiting for Jim to follow him inside.

"Morning." Jim waved with his good arm.

"Should you be out?" Rachel blurted.

"Nice to see you too." Jim started to chuckle, then grimaced, holding his side.

In a flash, she was on her feet and hurrying over to him. "You shouldn't be out."

"It's my ribs that hurt, not the rest of me, and last time I looked, I don't need my ribs to drive. Though Mom did insist I take the more comfortable Edge instead of the truck."

"Glad to see you're okay," her mom called from the kitchen.

"Thank you, ma'am." Smiling quickly at her mom, he glanced at Rachel, his gaze softened and she knew what was coming. Very slowly, he leaned in and gave her a soft kiss on the temple. "I can't bend any lower, or I'd give you a proper good morning kiss."

She didn't have to look over her shoulder to know her mother was watching and probably smiling too. Pushing up on her tippy toes, she gave his lips a gentle peck. "Good morning."

How Jim wished he could bend over, pull her in close, and give her a real kiss. And not just for her mother's sake. Last night, the way she'd held his hand in the ER, refused to leave his side, and hovered over him like a mother hen, everything felt so very real and not at all for show.

After spending most of the night on the recliner so he didn't have to move much, thinking about his life, the directions it had taken, leaving California and the high stress work that had ruled his every day and night, and how he'd wound up back in the one place he swore he never wanted to see again, one thing struck him very acutely. Never in the two years he'd dated Blair, or the months engaged to her, not even when planning their lives together, did he ever feel the way Rachel made him feel. Could it be as simple as the old cliché, there's no place like home?

"Come on," Rachel nudged him gently into the living room. "You should sit."

"My legs are fine."

She rolled her eyes at him, and then one hand on her hip, gave him a look that should have made any mere mortal whither.

"Okay. I'll sit."

"The recliner will be more comfortable."

"On that," he nodded, "we can agree."

He was just easing himself back, trying very hard not to show how damn much it hurt when Rachel's phone pinged once, twice, and three times, back-to-back.

Her gaze darted from him to the other side of the room and back.

"Go. I'm fine."

Waiting another second to make sure he was indeed fine; she darted to her purse on the sofa table and flipped through messages.

"Everything okay?" He didn't like the frown deepening between her eyes.

Slowly walking toward him, she continued to stare at her phone.

"Rach?"

She sank into the sofa beside him "Sorry. I've got a family I'm having a hard time helping."

"Tell me about it."

Her gaze lifted to meet his, and she blew out a sigh. "Most of the time, we're trying to protect kids from their parents. I hate to have to say this, but we don't always get to swoop in and save the kids from a troubled home life. Too often we spend time coaching the children on how not to aggravate the parents so they don't get hurt."

"That's crazy." Other words came to mind but none he could use without his mother threatening to wash his mouth out with soap, no matter how old he was.

"There's so much about the system that can be frustrating. Sometimes, some of us bend the rules."

"Bend?"

Her lips pressed tightly together, her shoulder dipped, and then she heaved a sigh. "You might say that there may have been a time or two when a social worker might take an injured kid in their own vehicle for… treatment."

"Some as in you?"

Again, her shoulder lifted, and her head tipped to meet it. "Maybe."

"Rach…" He struggled with how to say what he was thinking without coming off as a jerk. "Violent parents, taking kids without approval, you mentioned the other day tracking folks down on the streets if that's where they're smoking crack. Is your work always this dangerous?"

Her hesitation to respond told him more than he wanted to know.

"What's happening now?"

She glanced at her phone. "I have one case. The son is about to age out of the system. Not that it's been able to help much so far. He's schizophrenic, doesn't like taking his meds, and has a drug abuse problem. Whenever he gets into a placement to steady his meds and clean him up, they let him out and it starts all over again."

"Like now?"

Her head bobbed. "It's just the mom and a little sister. When he's in a good place, he's a sweet boy."

"But when he's not?"

"Mom just texted me that he left the house this afternoon and hasn't come home. She's worried. Actually, she's scared. She says that he's arguing with the voices."

"Man." Eyes closed, he relaxed fingers that had tightened into a fist. "Now what?"

"I'll make some calls tomorrow. Try a little harder to get him placement for evaluation before it escalates any more."

"What is it they say the definition of crazy is?"

"I know, doing the same thing over and over but expecting different results. It's all I can do. I can't fix everything, and I certainly can't cure schizophrenia."

"Sorry. I didn't mean—"

"No." She reached out and touched his arm. "When I can fix a situation, help a troubled mom, reach a lost kid, it's a euphoria like you wouldn't believe."

He felt his mouth tip in a slight smile. "You always loved straightening out messes. As I remember, the more chaotic and impossible the situation, the more drawn to it you were. I guess you still are."

"Most social workers, we thrive creating calm from chaos."

Holding his side, he stretched his arm and took hold of her hand. "You, Rachel Sweet, are amazing."

CHAPTER THIRTEEN

Rachel triple-checked the documents spread across the kitchen table—birth certificate, driver's license, social security card. "Do you think we need anything else?"

"We're getting a marriage license, not applying for top-secret clearance," Jim teased from the doorway, his bruised ribs still evident in the careful way he moved.

Gathering everything into a neat stack and sliding it into a folder, she willed her hands not to betray the nerves whirling about inside her. This was happening. Today. The first formal step toward their arrangement.

"Ready?" Jim dangled his car keys.

"As I'll ever be," she tried for lightness in her tone, worried she sounded more like a sailor about to walk the plank.

The drive into town was quiet. Almost too quiet, but she couldn't find anything to say that wouldn't betray her nerves. She fidgeted with the edge of the folder. They really were going to do this.

Just as they reached the edge of town, instead of continuing towards the courthouse, Jim made an unexpected turn, pulling into the nearly empty parking area by the park.

Confused, she glanced in his direction and pointed down the street. "Have you forgotten the courthouse is that way?"

"Nope." He cut the engine and turned to her, a serious yet gentle expression in his blue eyes. "Trust me?"

"Is it too soon to say I do?" She hoped she achieved the teasing tone she aimed for.

Jim smiled at her choice of words, then reached over

and squeezed her hand before climbing out of the car. Rachel followed, confusion giving way to curiosity as he led her past the swing sets and picnic tables toward the far corner of the park.

Recognition dawned as they approached the old wooden teeter-totter. A little weathered, a little worn, but still standing after all these years.

"You remember?" Jim watched her face.

She laughed softly. "How could I forget? Eighth grade, Billy Tucker dared you to jump off when I was in the air."

"And I refused, so he called me chicken."

"Then I jumped off just to show him I could, and you crashed to the ground so hard you bit your tongue."

Jim's hand unconsciously touched his lower lip. "Bled all over my new shirt."

"And I felt so guilty I brought you pudding cups every day for a week."

They both laughed at the memory, then Jim gestured toward the old wooden plank. "Shall we?"

"Are you serious? With your ribs?"

"I'll manage. Carefully."

Shaking her head at his stubbornness, Rachel positioned herself on one end while Jim gingerly settled on the other, bringing her side up into the air. They balanced there, feet dangling, like kids playing hooky instead of adults about to get a marriage license. They teetered up, then down, gently, and when Jim winced at landing a little too hard on his feet, she shook her head. "That's enough reminiscing. Let's get going."

Climbing down, instead of going directly to the car, he took hold of her hand and tugged her to a nearby picnic table. He sat down at her side.

"So," Jim's voice took on a more serious tone, "I know none of this is… conventional. And I know it's only temporary." He paused, holding her gaze. "But you deserve more than walking into a clerk's office, getting a license like we're merely going fishing, and then wearing a cigar band for a wedding ring."

Before she could process, his other hand reached into

his pocket. He pulled out a small, dark velvet box. Her breath caught and her hand floated to her chest.

He didn't open it immediately, just held it, his gaze locked with hers, holding her other hand firmly. "Rachel Sweet," his voice came out low and steady despite the vulnerability she saw flicker in his eyes, "will you sort of marry me?"

She just stared, first at the box, then back at his face. Her mind went completely blank.

As he waited, lips pressed into a tense line gave way to a slow easy smile. "Should I get down on one knee?"

The image, the absurdity, the sweetness of it all, broke through her paralysis. A laugh escaped, shaky but genuine. "Don't you dare. Your ribs have been through enough." Their gazes locked, and she nodded. "Yes. I'll sort of marry you."

Relief washed over his face. He opened the box, revealing a single diamond nestled within a delicate swirl of gold, flanked by tiny sparkling chips. Carefully, he took the ring from the box.

"It's beautiful," she whispered as he slid it onto her finger. Briefly, she admired how the single stone caught the morning light beautifully. Not too flashy, not too small… just beautiful.

"I could have gotten something bigger, but I didn't think you'd like that. If you want, we could go shopping, get something… different."

Shaking her head, she gazed down at the ring, then lifted her eyes to meet his. "No," she whispered, her voice thick with emotion she hadn't expected. "This is perfect."

Just a few more days and the woman sitting in the passenger side of the car would be Jim's *sort of* wife. The way she clutched the folder that now held the marriage license they'd applied for, he was pretty convinced that Rachel Sweet was feeling the pressure of the moment as much as he was.

"Isn't that your mother?" Rachel squinted down the driveway at the figure leaving the front porch.

It took him until they got a little closer to confirm. "Wonder what she's doing here?"

As soon as they came to a stop, Jim hopped out of the car, trotted around the front to catch the door for Rachel, then met his mom by her truck.

Standing at the open driver's door, her hand across the top, his mother smiled at him. "I spoke with Alice. Since y'all are in a sure fired hurry to get married, we figured with your ribs, you'd sleep better here on a real bed than on our recliner, so I dropped your stuff off." Shifting slightly, she flashed a wide smile and waved in Rachel's direction.

Jim felt his brows furrow. Was his mother actually for the first time ever in his entire life, suggesting he cohabitate with a female before standing in front of a preacher?

"Alice has plenty of space, and since y'all will be living here for a bit anyhow." His mom shrugged, stepped forward, kissed him on the cheek then stepped back. "I have to run. If I forgot anything, just give me a jingle and I'll send someone over with it."

He had no idea if he was confused, stunned, or sound asleep and dreaming. All he could think was that old joke, here's your hat what's your hurry, as someone shoves him, and his hat, out the front door. "Thanks."

Rachel looked up at him as if he'd sprouted a third eye.

The truck door slammed, the engine roared to life, and with a smile and a wave, his mother was kicking up dust behind her.

"That was a little odd." Rachel stared after the truck.

"My thoughts as well." Jim nodded, then, heaving a slow sigh, shrugged and turned. "Let's see what she brought."

One foot inside the doorway and it was obvious the place was bustling a bit more than usual. From the second floor, Carson called out something Jim didn't quite understand, then a second later, Jess could be heard answering something about needing more hangers.

"What the heck?" Rachel headed for the stairs, crossing

paths with her mom.

Arms burdened with a bundle of linens, Alice Sweet smiled at them. "Just going to toss these in the washing machine and then I'll change the sheets on the bed."

Before anyone could ask, she was through the kitchen and out of earshot.

Jim shrugged again and the two went up the stairs. In the middle of the hall, clothing draped over Jess's arm and Carson carrying a pile of folded shirts, the two stood, kissing.

"Get a room," Rachel teased, holding back a laugh.

"That's what we're doing." Carson winked at his wife and held up the shirts, his gaze looking briefly over his sister's shoulder down the stairs. "Like we agreed. The master is better for you guys."

"Apparently," Jess shifted the clothes to both arms, "your mothers agree because Alice has been up here directing the move and dusting after us."

Carson stood in the doorway of his old room and spoke to Jim. "Your mom left a couple of suitcases in there. I suggest you check with the future misses about how much closet space she's going to let you have before you start unpacking."

He'd never been in the Sweet master bedroom. Having grown up nearby and being similar in age to the boys, he'd been upstairs plenty of time, but never in the master. "This feels weird."

"Which part?" Rachel rolled her eyes skyward and walked into the bedroom.

The mattress was stripped, drawers were open and empty, and the closet didn't look big enough to hold a fraction of the clothes he'd left behind in California. Not that he'd need most of his custom wardrobe here in ranch country—those clothes could stay behind in California. In the corner of the room, his two suitcases sat side by side. *Side by side.* His eyes drifted to the bed. If getting a license to wed wasn't serious enough, staring at the bed he and Rachel would be sharing in a few days really drove the situation home.

At his side, Rachel stared at the king-size bed, her expression unreadable.

"It's a nice room." His hand brushed against hers and she startled as if surprised there was someone else in the house. Not a good sign. The weight of the situation was clearly affecting her.

"Sorry. I guess I'm a little… edgy."

Considering he knew how he felt, he couldn't fault her for feeling…edgy. "How much closet space do you need?"

The way she looked at him, a smile barely reaching the corners of her mouth, he knew his effort to ease the tension had worked. At least a little.

"Hey," smiling widely, he flipped his hands up in the air, "I have an image to maintain."

Groaning, she gently slugged him in the shoulder. "Men. You can have the big closet. I'll use the little one in the bathroom."

"A woman who believes in sharing is a woman after my own heart."

Now she grinned in earnest, shook her head, and turned away. "I'll get clean sheets for you."

Rooted to the carpet, he looked around the room. It was cozy, comfortable, and spacious. The problem, as he saw it, Buckingham Palace wouldn't be big enough to make sharing with Rachel easy.

CHAPTER FOURTEEN

lice Sweet took a slow, satisfied breath, the scent of wildflowers and freshly mown grass filled her senses. Clint had truly outdone himself. The simple wooden backdrop he'd constructed under the ancient oak tree at the back of the house was more beautiful than she could have imagined. As soon as the sun starts its nightly descent, combined with Clint's handiwork, they'd have the perfect setting for the next Sweet wedding. Her Rachel was going to be a beautiful bride.

"Clint, it's just lovely." She walked to where he stood, hiding the extension cords for the strings of fairy lights woven through the branches. "I don't know how to thank you. This backdrop is more than I hoped for."

Clint tipped his hat. "The bones are my doing, but the fabric and lights," he gestured to the soft ivory material artfully draped around the wooden beams, "this is all Miss Jillian." He chuckled. "She had strong opinions on how it should hang."

"I bet she did." Alice smiled. That sounded exactly like her daughter. Between Clint's sturdy craftsmanship and Jillian's eye for elegance, they'd created a little bit of magic right here in their backyard. It was perfect for Rachel and Jim. Simple, heartfelt, and surrounded by the land they all loved. The only thing missing would be Charlie to walk Rachel down the aisle.

Taking a step back, Clint nodded at the final results and once again tipped his hat. "I've got things to tend to before the festivities begin."

"You'll be finished in time for the ceremony." It wasn't really a question. "You're almost part of the family."

"Thank you, ma'am." Something she couldn't quite read flashed in his eyes. "I'll do my best."

The man who had been a savior to the Sweet family disappeared into the barn and Alice spun around for one more look at the beautiful setting, then glanced up at the lights in the tree. "Oh, Charlie. You always thought Jim would be the one. How I wish you could be here to see for yourself." Blowing a soft kiss into the air, she turned and walked back to the house. She had a wedding to dress for.

Had she completely lost her mind? Rachel stood in front of the mirror in the same room she'd slept in for most of her childhood. The same room that, for the last few days, had been only a few feet from the master bedroom where Jim had been sleeping. In a simple white mid-length dress, she felt like a bride from the fifties. Except this wasn't technically for real. Technically. She'd be legally wed, and sharing her life—and bed—for one whole year with a man who could make her heart race, and her palms sweat. She had to be out of her mind. That was the only explanation for going through with this insane plan.

"You look stunningly beautiful." Her mother stood staring at her with so much love and pride in her eyes that Rachel almost cried at how her mother's heart would break when one year from now all of this would come to an end.

Trying not to sigh, who was she kidding? Her heart was the one that would break when Jim Henderson once again walked out of her life.

Jillian appeared in the doorway. "Are you two going to stand up here looking at yourselves in the mirror all day, or are we having a wedding?"

Nodding, Alice Sweet took a step in retreat. "I'd better go take my seat. You know your dad is going to be at your side with every step."

It wasn't a question really, but Rachel nodded anyway.

As soon as her mother was out the door and down the

hall, Jillian met Rachel's eyes. "You still want to do this?"

Did she? Of course she did. The ranch needed the money. It was her duty. And truthfully, grateful to have him back in her life, she'd take whatever time with Jim she could get. "I do."

Jillian giggled. "Remember that."

Outside, the sky lit up in hues of fiery orange and soft lavender as Rachel made her way down the short aisle to stand beside Jim, tucking her hand securely in the crook of his arm. The simple vows, spoken with a surprising depth of sincerity from the local Justice of the Peace Alice had rustled up, still echoed in her ears. His ring felt solid, a tangible weight on her finger, a constant reminder of this wild, improbable turn her life had taken.

Under the nearby open-sided tent, tables were laden with smoked brisket, corn bread, creamed corn, and all the other fixings of a proper Texas celebration. Fairy lights twinkled, mimicking the stars beginning to prick the darkening sky. The reception was small, just their two families, more of a party than a reception really. Their parents chatted joyfully, Mason darted between tables, proudly showing off a frog he'd caught, and her brothers, with their wives, seemed to be in a contest of who could tell the most embarrassing childhood story about her or Jim. The only person missing was Kade. Even though this wasn't a real wedding, she still wished her eldest brother could be here to give her a hug and remind her to *suck it up, buttercup*.

Her mother's voice boomed through the speaker system set up. "I'd like to propose a toast." Champagne glasses were raised. "To Rachel and Jim. What took you so long?" The crowd roared with laughter, forcing Alice to raise her hand to quiet everyone. "Seriously. May your life together be filled with as much love and laughter as you've brought to ours."

Glasses clinked and Aunt Vicki, acting as photographer, insisted they link elbows in a traditional sipping photo. Rachel met Jim's gaze. It all felt so real.

On his feet, Jim's dad also raised his glass and the

crowd fell silent. "Like Alice and Charlie, your mother and I always thought you and Rachel were meant to be. Honestly," he turned and winked at his wife, "I'm surprised your mother didn't drag a preacher to the ranch with your suitcases, just to make sure no one changed their minds."

The crowd chuckled in varying ranges of amused laughter.

"Too many years of love and happiness." Mr. Henderson's eyes sparkled as he drank to his son and new bride. Just like a real wedding. Rachel didn't want to think ahead to a year from now.

Next, her aunt ushered them over to the cake—a simple single tiered creation with the same topper that had been on Jim's parents' cake. Jim's hand felt warm over hers as they made the first cut, the scent of vanilla and buttercream filling the air. Each breaking off a small piece, she was first to hold the morsel to his lips. The crowd once again erupting with laughter as she accidentally nipped the tip of his nose with a dollop of icing. The chuckle rumbling low in Jim's throat brought a smile to her face.

He swallowed and lifted his piece to her lips. Leaning in, he whispered, "Relax," kissed the tip of her nose, placed the morsel in her mouth. As she closed her lips to swallow, he leaned in impossibly closer and tenderly kissed her. For something just for show, everything felt incredibly real.

Another hour of chatting, visiting, posing for more photos for her aunt and their moms to gather plates. Instinctively, Rachel rose to help.

"Oh no you don't, young lady," Alice gently but firmly shooed her back towards Jim. Jim's mom echoed the sentiment from across the table. "You are not cleaning up after your own reception."

"Besides," her mother glanced over at her sister Liz and gave her a thumbs up, "it's about time you said your goodnights and go make your own music."

A blush crept up Rachel's neck at the not-so-subtle implication.

Jim stood, his hand finding hers, his thumb brushing over her new ring. His gaze met hers and she knew what he was thinking, no postponing the inevitable.

Before she could turn, chairs were kicking back, guests were scurrying about, and within moments, everyone was lined up on either side of the walkway to the house, creating an archway of sparklers for them to walk under. Hurrying past everyone, they scurried up the steps and into the house. She didn't dare look back or she might fall completely apart.

The screen door banged shut behind them, the sudden quiet of the house a stark contrast to the boisterous well wishes still echoing from the yard.

Still holding her hand, Jim glanced over his shoulder. "I may be wrong, but I have a feeling that the party isn't going to end any time soon."

She glanced out the window and smiled. "I have a feeling you're absolutely correct."

They stood for another few moments in awkward silence. "I suppose we should head upstairs. It wouldn't look right if anyone came into the house for something and found the two of us watching the party like a couple of kids with their noses pressed against the candy store window."

"No." She didn't let go but inched back half a step. "I don't suppose it would."

Falling into step beside each other, they made their way upstairs, their steps slowing as they reached the master bedroom door, Jim tugging her to a stop.

"Is something wrong?" Eyes filled with confusion stared up at him.

"No. Just a little tradition." Ignoring his still pained ribs, he bent and scooped her into his arms before she could react.

"Jim Henderson, what in the world do you think you're doing?" she giggled, her arms instinctively going around his neck.

"Carrying my bride over the threshold, of course." He

took the first step. "Even a *sort of* bride deserves that much, don't you think?"

The laughter had faded from her eyes, replaced by something softer, more vulnerable. He could feel the gentle thud of her heart against his chest.

"You can put me down now."

"Oh. Right." Releasing her slowly, as much to protect his sore ribs as to feel her closeness just a moment longer, he carefully inched back before he did something really stupid. Like take her in his arms and kiss her not for show, but the way she deserved to be kissed. The way he'd been dying to kiss her since they'd made that foolish deal that wasn't much of a joke to him.

"So," Rachel finally spoke, her voice a little breathy as she smoothed down her dress, her gaze fixed on the large bed.

"So," Jim echoed, suddenly acutely aware of the silence stretching between them. He glanced around the room—their room now—taking in the small touches that had appeared since he'd left earlier in the day. Someone had scattered rose petals across the comforter. A bottle of champagne sat in an ice bucket on the dresser, two glasses beside it.

"I think we're being set up," Rachel laughed nervously, gesturing toward the romantic additions.

"Your family doesn't do anything halfway, do they?" Jim smiled, hopefully easing some of the tension.

"We should probably change." Rachel's voice caught slightly.

"Of course." Jim nodded. "I'll just…" he gestured vaguely toward the bathroom, grabbing his pajama pants and t-shirt from where he'd left them folded on a chair earlier.

In the bathroom, Jim changed quickly, splashing cold water on his face and staring at himself in the mirror. Married. He was married—sort of. The weight of the gold band on his own finger felt surprisingly right. Taking a deep breath, with no clue what the next year was going to bring, he gave himself a short nod in the mirror and opened the door.

Rachel stood by the open door to the larger walk-in closet. "You didn't unpack?"

"Actually," he inched closer, "I took the bathroom closet."

Her smile bloomed and something in his chest shifted. Nothing seemed as important as seeing her happy.

Jim shrugged, trying to appear casual. "The walk-in made more sense for you."

Something flickered in her eyes—surprise, perhaps, or gratitude. "Thank you."

The silence that followed was charged with a different kind of tension than before.

"I'd better change." She grabbed a pile of clothing from the bed and hurried into the bathroom. A moment later she appeared in a pair of pink sweatpants with a long-sleeved cotton t-shirt with moons and stars in sparkles. Nothing had ever looked better.

"Well." Sucking in a deep breath, Jim gestured toward the bed. "Should we…"

"Right." Rachel nodded, hanging her dress and closing the closet door. "Which side do you prefer?"

"I usually sleep on the left, but with these ribs…" he touched his side gingerly, "maybe the right would be better for now."

"Perfect. I always sleep on the left anyway."

They approached the bed from opposite sides, each pulling back the covers and carefully removing the rose petals. Jim caught Rachel's eye as she scooped up a handful, and they both broke into laughter.

"My mother," Rachel giggled.

"At least there's no heart made out of towels," Jim countered, making her laugh harder.

The shared moment eased the awkwardness as they slid under the covers, each staying carefully on their respective sides. Jim reached over and turned off the lamp on his nightstand, plunging the room into darkness save for the faint moonlight filtering through the curtains.

They lay there, not touching, both staring up at the ceiling.

"This is weird, isn't it?" Rachel finally whispered into the darkness.

"A little," Jim admitted, turning his head to look at her profile. "But not in a bad way."

She turned to face him, her features softened by shadows. "No?"

"No," he said with quiet conviction. "Just… new."

Another silence fell, more comfortable this time.

"Jim?" Rachel's voice was barely audible.

"Hmm?"

"Thank you for today. For making it feel…" she paused, searching for the right word, "real."

No way could he tell her that for him everything was becoming very real. "My pleasure, Mrs. Henderson." His thumb brushing lightly over her knuckles.

"Goodnight, Mr. Sweet." He felt rather than saw her smile in the darkness.

Jim chuckled. "That's not how it works."

"I know," she said, a teasing note in her voice. "But it got you to laugh."

Their hands still joined atop the covers, as sleep began to claim him, Jim realized that whatever this arrangement was—real, pretend, or somewhere in between—it felt dangerously close to right.

CHAPTER FIFTEEN

Rachel leaned toward the dresser mirror, carefully applying lipstick. Satisfied, she reached for her small pearl earrings—professional but not flashy, perfect for an impromptu visit to the county health department.

Over the last several days, they had settled into a strange yet comfortable rhythm of married life. Shared breakfasts, brief touches as they passed each other or sat together at mealtime, and—most important—careful navigation of the bathroom schedule. It was all so... domestic.

She fastened the second earring just as the click of the bathroom door opening made her turn. Jim emerged a towel slung low on his hips, another one vigorously rubbing his damp hair. Water droplets clung to his broad shoulders and chest. Rachel's mouth went suddenly dry. She swallowed hard, willing herself not to smudge her freshly applied lipstick. He looked... good. Too good for seven in the morning.

"Sorry." The amusement in his eyes suggested he wasn't entirely sorry at all. "Forgot to grab my underwear."

"No problem." Despite the sudden flutter in her stomach, her voice sounded impressively steady. She moved slightly to the side, giving him access to the dresser while steadfastly keeping her eyes on her own reflection.

Jim reached past her for his clothes, his arm briefly brushing hers. The casual contact—skin against skin—sent a ripple of awareness through her that was anything but casual. The second towel now draped around his neck, he held an armful of clothes and paused in the bathroom doorway, looking at her over his shoulder. "Isn't today your work-from-home day?"

She nodded, turning back to the mirror to fuss with an earring that didn't need fussing. "Yes, but I haven't been able to get anywhere with the county health department over that case I told you about, the one that's escalating. I thought if I showed up in person, maybe I could actually get something done." She picked up her purse. "And while I'm in the city, maybe do a little window shopping. Clear my head."

Jim leaned against the door jamb, his eyes never leaving hers. "Want some company?"

The offer caught her by surprise. "For real?"

"Why not? There's nothing pressing on my work schedule today. Could be nice to get out of the house for a bit."

Rachel hesitated. She'd been mentally preparing herself for a potentially frustrating morning of bureaucracy and red tape. Having Jim there would be... a complication. Or a comfort. Maybe both. "I could be waiting for hours. These government offices aren't exactly known for their efficiency."

Jim shrugged, the movement causing the towel to slip slightly lower on his hips. Rachel quickly averted her eyes.

"Then we can wait together," he shrugged simply. He pushed off the door jamb and walked towards the closet. "Give me five minutes to find something that doesn't scream bruised ribs and impending doom."

She watched him go, a small smile playing on her lips. He really was something else. Giving in, she nodded, more to herself than to him. "Okay, Henderson. But don't say I didn't warn you."

Twenty minutes later, they were in Jim's car heading toward the county seat. Rachel had her case files balanced on her lap, reviewing notes and mentally preparing for the meeting she hoped to have. The Torres case had been weighing on her heavily—seventeen-year-old Michael struggling with schizophrenia, substance abuse issues, and a recent expulsion from his group home. His mother Maria was at her wit's end, especially concerned about Michael's younger sister Lily.

"You're worried about this one more than the others, aren't you?" Jim glanced her way, breaking the comfortable silence between them.

Rachel nodded, not looking up from her notes. "When mental health and the system fail these kids, it's usually the families who bear the brunt. And sometimes…"

"Sometimes it gets dangerous," Jim finished for her, his gaze narrowed, focused on the road ahead, but the tightness in his jaw reflected his intensity and had nothing to do with the road and everything to do with her and this troubled family.

"Yeah." She closed the folder with a sigh. "Michael's a good kid underneath it all. He just can't seem to stay on his medication, and without it, the voices take over. His mom called yesterday saying he's been arguing with himself more and more and staying out of the house longer and longer. She knows it won't take much to make him snap and is terrified anything she does or says might be the catalyst."

"I had no idea the system was so broken." Jim reached across the console, his hand covering hers briefly. "You're doing everything you can."

"I hope it's enough," she murmured.

The county building came into view, a squat, utilitarian structure of brick and narrow windows. Jim found a parking spot easily—one of the few perks of arriving early.

As they walked toward the entrance, Rachel mentally rehearsed her argument for expedited services for the Benson family. She needed a miracle to bump Michael to the top of the list for immediate services.

Inside, they maneuvered down the corridor. Rachel gripped the handle to her bag so tightly her nails dug into her palm. She had to find the right words, how to explain to the people with the power that Michael needed help—real help—before something terrible happened.

Just as she reached the correct door, her phone rang. Handing her bag with all her files to Jim, she dug it out of her purse, checking the screen. "It's Kathy Benson. She never calls this early," she muttered to herself, anxiety immediately spiking. This couldn't be good.

Jim watched as Rachel's expression shifted from professional calm to urgent focus in a heartbeat.

"Kathy, slow down. Take a deep breath." Her voice remained steady despite the tension in her posture. "Where's Michael now? …. And Lily? She's with you?… Okay. Stay put." Phone to her ear, she turned, moving quickly down the hall. "I'm on my way. Just hang on." Ending the call, she turned to Jim. "We have to go. Now."

"What's happened?" Jim matched her stride.

"Michael—the kid I'm so worried about—is having an episode. His mom says the voices are telling him that he has to save his sister." Rachel pushed through the door, her steps quickening. "They're barricaded in the bathroom and he's tearing up the apartment."

"Are the police on the way?"

Rachel shook her head. "Kathy's afraid of what he'll do if he sees the police. He hasn't had good results with them."

The urgency in her voice propelled Jim forward, all thoughts of a leisurely morning forgotten. "I'm driving."

They reached the car in record time. As Rachel buckled in, she was already making another call, her fingers moving with practiced efficiency.

"Marty, it's Rachel Sweet. I'm heading to the Benson residence now. EDP situation, seventeen-year-old male, schizophrenic, off meds, currently experiencing paranoid delusions." She rattled off an address. "Mother and younger sister barricaded in bathroom. I need backup, but no sirens, no uniforms if possible. He's scared, not dangerous—at least not intentionally."

Jim pulled onto the main road, pressing the gas harder than strictly necessary. Rachel's calm professional demeanor impressed him, but he could see the worry in her eyes, the slight tremor in her hands as she ended the call.

"This Marty—police?" he asked, taking a sharp turn onto the highway.

"Crisis response team. Michael only trusts me, but…" She glanced over at him. "This could get ugly."

Knowing ugly was her way of saying dangerous, all he could do was nod.

"Michael knows me. If I can get him talking, get him to focus on my voice instead of the ones in his head, we might be able to de-escalate."

"And if you can't?"

Rachel's silence was answer enough.

The apartment complex came into view—a weathered four-story building with peeling paint and a sign advertising "affordable living." Jim pulled into the first available spot, barely putting the car in park before Rachel was out the door.

"Apartment 412," she called over her shoulder, already heading for the stairs.

Jim caught up in two long strides. As they rushed up the stairwell, the sound of shouting became audible—a young man's voice, alternating between anger and fear.

"You're lying! She's not Lily! Where's my real sister?"

The crash of something breaking punctuated the question.

Rachel paused at the landing, her hand on Jim's arm. "You'll need to stay out of the way. I can't risk your presence adding to his fears, understood?"

The authority in her voice—so different from the woman who'd been fussing with her earrings less than an hour ago—stirred something in him. Pride, respect, and an unmistakable surge of protectiveness.

"Understood," he said, though every instinct told him to put himself between her and whatever danger lay behind that door.

The apartment door was ajar, hanging awkwardly from one hinge. Rachel pushed it open slowly. "Michael?" she called, her voice deliberately calm and warm. "It's Rachel. Rachel Sweet. I'm coming in, okay?"

The shouting paused briefly. Jim stood in the doorway glancing into a small living area that looked like a tornado had struck. Furniture overturned, glass shattered across the floor, picture frames smashed. A tall, lanky teenager stood by the window, a little girl, maybe four or five, clutched against him in one arm, the other hand gripping a bat. "Stay away. I need to save Lily."

The urge to rush in and snatch the little girl away almost overwhelmed him, only Rachel's words—stay back—kept his feet rooted in place.

Michael's eyes were wild, darting around the room as if tracking invisible movements. Sweat plastered his dark hair to his forehead. "They took Lily. They replaced her."

"No, Michael. That's not true." Rachel stepped forward carefully, hands open at her sides. "Lily is fine. She's your sister. The same sister you've always had."

"Please, Michael." In tears, his mother stood hunched, hugging herself. "She's your sister. She loves you."

"No! She has to die for Lily to come back. They told me."

Jim remained by the door, taking in the scene, assessing threats and exits. The bathroom door was off the hinges; the wood cracked in half. This kid had to have the strength of a legion of demons.

"Michael," Rachel continued, inching closer. "Remember what we talked about? About the voices? They lie to you."

"Mommy!" Squirming in her brother's grip, Lily began to cry. "I want Mommy."

"I'm here, baby." Kathy looked to Rachel then back to her daughter and son. "Please, Michael. Let me take Lily away."

"It's not Lily." Michael spun and placing one hand on the open window, swung a leg over the ledge.

"Michael," Rachel repeated with more calm than Jim would expect in this situation. "Tell me what you're thinking."

"We have to jump."

Kathy screamed, "No!"

Rachel waved her back and took a slow minced step forward. "Michael. You love your sister."

"This isn't my sister."

"Yes. Michael. I never lie to you. That's Lily and she's scared."

For a moment, Jim thought the kid was going to agree, see the errors of his way, but in a flash, he turned and now Lily was dangling from the window.

CHAPTER SIXTEEN

Panic, cold and sharp, clawed at Rachel's throat, but she shoved it down, forcing her voice to remain even, a calm anchor in the swirling chaos. Lily, a terrified child in Michael's agitated grip, dangled precariously from the fourth-story window. One wrong move, one shift in Michael's fractured reality, and the unthinkable would happen. "Michael, look at me. Ignore the voices. Look at me."

His eyes, wild and unfocused, flickered briefly to her face. His grip on Lily remained firm as the child dangled from the window, her small legs kicking in terrified desperation.

"Mommy!" Lily's cry pierced the air.

Kathy took a lurching step forward, but Rachel subtly raised her hand, stopping her. Any sudden movement might push Michael over the edge—literally.

"I know you love your sister," Rachel continued, inching closer. "I know you'd never hurt Lily. The real Lily."

Michael's face contorted with confusion. "This isn't—"

"It is," Rachel interrupted gently but firmly. "Look at her bracelet, Michael. The one on her wrist."

His gaze dropped momentarily to the beaded bracelet on Lily's tiny wrist.

"You made that for her," Rachel pressed, taking another careful step. "For her birthday. Remember? Green beads because it's her favorite color."

Something flickered across his face—a moment of clarity cutting through the delusion.

"These voices, Michael, they're confusing you. Making

you see things that aren't real. But I'm real. Lily is real." Rachel was close enough now that she could almost touch them. "And you don't want to hurt her. She needs you, Michael. She needs her big brother to bring her back inside where it's safe. Let me help you. Let's bring Lily back in."

Slowly, she extended her hands toward Lily. "Give her to me and then we'll figure this out. Together"

Time seemed to stretch as Michael stared at her, the battle behind his eyes visible in the rapid shifting of his expressions. Then, almost imperceptibly, he nodded.

"I'm going to take Lily now." With infinite care, she reached for the little girl. Michael's grip loosened further, allowing Rachel to slide her hands under Lily's arms. As soon as the child was inside, she clung to her desperately as Rachel pulled her away from the window and stumbled back, her heart hammering.

She spun around, her eyes finding Jim, who had remained a silent, steady presence by the doorway, his own face, a mask of controlled tension. She gestured for Jim to come close. Slowly, he moved beside her, gently taking Lily into his arms. Returning her focus to Michael, she kept her voice low, almost a whisper, and dared to face Jim. "Get her and Kathy out of here." She could see the objection forming in his eyes. "Please."

As Jim carried the sobbing child to Kathy, he gently urged them toward the door.

"But my boy," Kathy sobbed, clutching Lily to her chest.

"Is in the best possible hands," Jim's voice mirrored the same calm Rachel worked desperately to display. "We need to give Rachel space to help him."

As they disappeared into the hallway, Rachel took a deep breath, focusing entirely on the troubled young man.

Michael's expression shifted again—the momentary clarity disappearing as quickly as it had come. "No!" he shouted suddenly. "You tricked me!"

He lunged forward, but Rachel stood her ground. "Michael, no one is tricking you. I promised to help, and I will."

"The voices said you'd lie," he accused, half in and half out of the window. "They said everyone lies."

"Remember what Dr. Feldman told you? About how your brain sometimes plays tricks?"

Michael hesitated, and Rachel seized the opening. "You've been off your medication, haven't you?"

He nodded reluctantly. "They make everything fuzzy."

"I know." Rachel nodded. "But they also make the voices quiet."

For a moment, it seemed to be working. Michael's posture relaxed slightly, his eyes focusing more clearly on her face. Then the distant wail of sirens shattered the fragile calm. Michael's head snapped toward the sound, panic washing over his features. "They're coming for me! You called them!"

"No, Michael, I—"

But it was too late. Terror propelled him out the window, leaving him perched precariously on the narrow ledge outside.

"I have to get away," he babbled, his entire body trembling. "They'll lock me up again. They'll hurt me."

"Michael, please." Rachel slowly, carefully, leaned into the windowsill. "Come back inside. We can talk to them together. I won't let them hurt you."

The sirens grew louder, approaching the building. Michael pressed himself against the outer wall, edging further along the ledge.

"Rachel," Jim's voice, low and tense, came from behind her. He was supposed to be downstairs with Kathy and Lily. Safe from here. "The police are coming up the stairs."

Blast. None of this should have happened. "If the police burst in here, it'll push him over the edge. Literally. Explain the situation. Buy me some time."

The conflict in his eyes was palpable—the need to protect her warring with the understanding that she knew what she was doing. "Two minutes," he said finally. "Then I'm coming back, police or no police."

Rachel nodded once, already turning back to Michael.

"Michael," she called softly. "It's just you and me now."

"They're still coming," his voice was tight with panic.

"I know. But I'm not going anywhere," Rachel promised. "And I know how scared you are right now."

"You don't understand." Tears streamed down his face. "No one understands."

"Then help me understand. Tell me what the voices are saying."

Michael shook his head frantically. "You'll think I'm crazy."

"I don't think you're crazy, Michael. I think you need help. There's a difference."

The sirens stopped, the sudden silence almost more ominous than the wailing. Footsteps thundered up the stairwell.

Michael's panic visibly increased. "They're here!"

Without hesitation, Rachel climbed onto the windowsill. "I'm coming out there with you."

"What are you doing?" Michael's eyes widened in shock.

"I promised I wouldn't leave you," Rachel carefully maneuvered onto the narrow ledge beside him. "And I keep my promises."

The world suddenly, and frighteningly, tilted on its axis. One second Rachel was pleading with Michael from the safety of the room, the next she was swinging her legs out, settling beside him on that impossibly narrow fourth-story ledge. Jim's breath hitched; his heart hammered against his bruised ribs with a force that made him wince, a pain completely separate from the terror gripping him. He'd told her two minutes. It hadn't even been one.

He'd just reached the apartment doorway, Kathy and Lily safely on their way down with one of the officers who'd arrived, when he saw Rachel make her move. His instinct was to yell, to rush forward, but some deeper, horrified part of him knew any sudden action could send them both tumbling.

"What the hell is she doing?" one of the remaining officers muttered, his voice tight with a tension that mirrored Jim's own. His hand hovered near his radio, his stance alert.

"We've got eyes on the subject, young male on the ledge, fourth floor. Child and mother are clear. Social worker is on the ledge with suspect."

"Her name is Rachel Sweet. The boy is Michael Benson, seventeen, schizophrenic. He's hearing voices."

The officer nodded. As he repeated the information into the radio Jim stepped fully into the room, his gaze locked on Rachel and Michael. He had to trust her, trust her training, her connection with this kid. But damn, it was hard. He could hear her voice, incredibly calm, a low murmur against the sudden, awful silence that had fallen now that the sirens were cut. He couldn't make out the words from here, but he could see the subtle shift in Michael's posture as she spoke, the way his head tilted slightly towards her.

Transmission done, the officer started to inch past Jim, and he shot out an arm, barring the officer's path. "Hold it. She said if you go near that window, you'll spook him. Make it worse."

The officer hesitated, his eyes flicking from Jim to the precarious scene on the ledge. "Sir, my priority is their safety."

"So is hers," Jim bit out, never taking his eyes off Rachel. "She's an experienced social worker. This is what she does. Just… give her a chance." He willed the man to understand, to see the quiet strength in Rachel, the almost hypnotic way she was engaging Michael.

On a sigh, the officer nodded, but like Jim, he seemed ready to pounce.

Every muscle in Jim's body was coiled tight. He was useless here, a spectator to the most terrifying moment of his life. He could only watch, his own breathing shallow, as Rachel continued her quiet conversation. He saw her hand move, a slow, deliberate gesture, and then, unbelievably,

Michael's head turned slightly, his gaze seeming to focus on her.

Time warped, stretching and compressing. The silence in the room was thick, broken only by the faint sounds from the street below and the almost inaudible murmur of Rachel's voice. Jim found himself cataloging every detail—the way the slight breeze ruffled Rachel's hair, the rigid set of Michael's shoulders, the sheer, terrifying drop beneath them.

Then, a movement. Michael shifted, his body angling infinitesimally back towards the window opening. Jim's heart stuttered. Was this it? Was she getting through?

Slowly, agonizingly, Michael swung one leg back inside. Then the other. He was in, collapsing onto the floor, his shoulders shaking with sobs.

The officer moved in, another only steps behind him. With a quiet professionalism, they approached Michael, speaking to him in low, reassuring tones. Paramedics, who must have arrived with the police, were being ushered in.

Rachel remained on the ledge a moment longer, her face pale in the afternoon light. Jim darted across the room, past the officers, the paramedics, and the troubled youth who had set the terrifying scene in motion.

Arms outstretched, Jim grabbed hold of her wrist. With what looked like a monumental effort, one arm on the windowsill, the other still firmly in his grip, she maneuvered herself back through the window, her legs unsteady as she stepped onto the solid floor.

An overwhelming flood of relief threatened to buckle his own knees. He didn't say anything, couldn't. He just pulled her into his arms, holding her tight, feeling the tremors that now racked her body. He buried his face in her hair, inhaling the scent of her, the scent of sunshine and unimaginable courage. The world narrowed to this single point, this woman in his arms, safe.

When he finally eased her back, his hands still gripping her shoulders as if afraid she might disappear, he searched her face. "Rachel..."

She looked up at him, a shaky smile touching her lips.

He couldn't stop himself. He leaned down and kissed her. It wasn't for show, not for the town, not for family. This was for him, for her. A kiss that poured out every ounce of terror, relief, and a love so fierce it stole his breath. It was a promise, a claim, a desperate acknowledgment of everything she'd become to him in such a short, chaotic time.

Pulling back, resting his forehead against hers, he let out a ragged breath. "Please," he murmured, his voice hoarse, "tell me this isn't just another day at the office?"

CHAPTER SEVENTEEN

The Sweet kitchen hummed with its usual evening chaos—a symphony of sizzling pans, clattering plates, and overlapping conversations. Hours had passed since the terrifying incident at the Benson apartment, hours filled with police reports, concerned check-ins with Kathy, and a quiet, almost numb drive back to the ranch with Jim. Now, Rachel stood at the counter slicing tomatoes, the familiar rhythms of dinner preparation a welcome anchor after the day she'd had.

"Pass the salt?" her mom called from the stove, barely looking up from the sauce she was stirring.

Jim, who had somehow been seamlessly absorbed into the family's cooking routine, reached for the shaker and handed it over, his fingers brushing Rachel's arm as he moved past her. The brief contact sent a warm flutter down her spine, a reaction that had nothing to do with the day's adrenaline and everything to do with the man himself.

She'd given a brief, sanitized version of the day to her family—a difficult case, a teen in crisis, resolved safely— and left it at that. No one else in this busy kitchen knew what they'd experienced hours earlier—the terrifying moments on that ledge, the desperate relief of safety, the kiss that had changed everything.

Stepping aside, Jim leaned against the counter, not saying much, but every few minutes, his eyes would find hers across the busy kitchen, reminding her of his earlier unwavering support. Not just his physical presence at the Benson home, standing as a silent guard, but the absolute, unquestioning belief he'd shown in her ability to handle Michael—it had been a lifeline.

"Earth to Rachel." Jillian nudged her with an elbow. "You're butchering that poor tomato."

Rachel glanced down, realizing she'd been mindlessly slicing the same spot. "Sorry." She readjusted her grip on the knife, pretending not to notice the way Jim smiled at her sister calling her out on her distraction.

"Rachel, honey, can you grab another can of diced tomatoes from the pantry?" Her mother waved toward the far corner of the kitchen. "Maybe two."

"Sure." She set down the knife and headed toward the spacious walk-in pantry that the family joked held enough food to support half the town if Armageddon struck. Flipping on the light, she scanned the shelves, quickly spotting the tomato section.

"Need help finding something?"

The soft creak of the pantry door opening behind her made her jump slightly. She turned to find Jim in the doorway, his tall frame nearly filling the space. Holding up a can, she shook her head.

He stepped inside, closing the door partway behind him. "I…I wanted a minute alone with you. This seemed like my best chance."

The pantry suddenly felt much smaller, the air between them charged with unspoken words. Rachel set the can down on a shelf, her pulse quickening.

"Are you okay?" he asked, his voice low, meant only for her.

She managed a small nod, her throat suddenly tight. "Yeah. Just… processing."

The space suddenly felt charged, electric. "About earlier…" he began, his voice even rougher than before.

She knew he wasn't talking about Michael, or the ledge, or the police. Her own heart began to hammer a frantic rhythm against her ribs. "I was okay, Jim. Really. You didn't need to worry."

Jim stepped closer, the space between them narrowing to inches. "It didn't worry me. It terrified me. Not because I doubted you," his gaze dropped to her lips, then back to her eyes, "because I couldn't bear the thought of losing you."

"Oh." Her heartbeat just a little faster, her mouth went suddenly dry, and try as she might, words simply didn't come.

His hand came up to brush a strand of hair from her face, the gesture achingly tender.

Rachel leaned into his touch, her eyes closing briefly.

"About earlier. The kiss."

"I understand." Her eyes opened to meet his. "People do unlikely things in stressful situations."

"Or when they're in love."

Her breath caught. "When what?"

"When they're in love," Jim repeated, more firmly this time. His gaze remained locked with hers. "I didn't kiss you because of the stress or the relief or any of that. I kissed you because I'm in love with you."

The vulnerability in his eyes undid her. All these weeks of careful distance, of reminding herself that this wasn't real, that his heart belonged elsewhere—and he'd been falling just as surely as she had.

"Funny thing," she tried to keep her tone light, "it seems that I've fallen in love with you too."

A smile pulled at his lips. "Funny." He lowered his head, his lips hovering a breath away from hers. "It's always been you, Rach. Only you."

Just like earlier, his mouth pressed hard against hers, and every nerve in her body came to life.

The sound of a throat clearing filled the space, breaking them apart. Jillian stood in the pantry doorway, one eyebrow raised, a smirk playing at her lips. "Mom sent me to find out what was taking so long."

Rachel felt a blush rise to her cheeks, but she didn't pull away from Jim. "We were just…"

"Right." Still grinning, Jillian shook her head, reached around them to grab two cans of tomatoes, and without another word, returned to the kitchen.

Both Rachel and Jim burst into giggles.

"I guess we'd better get back to dinner." Rachel forced herself to take a step in retreat.

"Right." He nodded. "Dinner."

Her cheeks tugged at her lips, her smiling stretching across her face. "And then… dessert."

Fingers threaded, they strolled out of the pantry. Life was about to get a whole lot sweeter.

All Jim could think was what a difference a day made. The bathroom door, which had previously represented a carefully negotiated boundary, now creaked open and closed with an easy familiarity.

Rachel moved about the room, her earlier tension replaced by a soft, contented glow that made his chest ache in the best possible way. She hummed a little tune as she brushed her hair, the lamplight catching the silver in her pearl earrings—the same ones she'd worn that morning, an eternity ago, before their world had tilted, then righted itself in a way he still couldn't quite believe.

Taking his turn in the bathroom, he changed into his usual pajama pants and tugged the t-shirt on as he walked back into the room.

Glancing his way as she pulled back the covers on her side of the bed, Rachel's eyes fell on the angry bruises surrounding his battered ribs. "Still sore?"

"Barely feel it," he lied. Watching her climb into her side of the bed, it struck him how quickly they'd established these small rituals, how easily they'd carved out space in each other's lives. Only tonight felt different—no more pretending, no more walls between them.

As they climbed in, instead of the usual careful retreat to their respective edges, a silent, mutual understanding drew them towards the middle. He settled onto his back, and without a word, Rachel turned onto her side, her head finding the curve of his good shoulder, her arm draping lightly across his chest. Her hair, smelling faintly of wildflowers, tickled his chin. He instinctively tightened his arm around her, pulling her closer, breathing in her scent. This felt… right. Impossibly, wonderfully right.

"You're quiet," she murmured, her breath soft against his neck.

"Just thinking," he admitted. All through dinner, washing dishes, the casual family conversation afterward, his mind had been racing, filled with possibilities he'd never considered before today.

"About?"

His fingers traced idle patterns along her arm, marveling at the softness of her skin, the easy intimacy they'd fallen into. How had he ever imagined this would be temporary? "Mostly about what comes next."

Rachel shifted, propping herself up on one elbow to look at him. In the soft glow of the bedside lamp, her eyes searched his face. "You haven't changed your mind, have you?"

The uncertainty in her voice tugged at something deep in his chest. Jim reached up, tucking a strand of hair behind her ear. "Not a chance. Not ever."

The smile that spread across her face was like sunrise— slow, beautiful, illuminating. She leaned down, pressing her lips gently against his. Jim's hand came up to cup the back of her neck, keeping her close as the kiss deepened, still marveling that he was allowed to do this now. That this wasn't for show or appearance, but because they'd made a vow, no longer a business deal for one year, but now it was understood they would love and honor till death do they part.

When she pulled back, he reveled in every detail of her face—the slight flush in her cheeks, the flecks of gold in her green eyes, the softness of her lips.

Jim shifted, sitting up a bit straighter against the pillows, organizing his thoughts. "I've been thinking about Michael and kids like him. The ones falling through the cracks."

"There are so many," Rachel said, a familiar sadness touching her eyes.

"Too many," Jim agreed. "And the system is broken. I saw that today." He paused, gathering his courage for what felt strangely like a second proposal. "I have resources,

Rachel. What if we used some of it to start a foundation?"

Her eyes widened. "A foundation?"

"Something to help these kids—a safe home, halfway house, outpatient therapy." His words came faster now, excitement building. "Whatever you think would make a real difference."

For a long moment, Rachel just stared at him, her lips slightly parted in surprise. The silence stretched, and doubt began to creep in.

"I've learned a lot since coming home. The business can run just fine without me. Don't get me wrong, I'll still go back from time to time to make sure all is as it should be, but I don't ever want to live for my job again. I could run this new foundation—with your guidance—and really make a difference. Is it a bad idea?" Uncertainty edged into his voice.

Then Rachel's face transformed, a smile blooming that rivaled the Texas sun. She leaned over him, her face hovering just above his, close enough that he could feel her breath on his lips.

"No, Mr. Henderson," she whispered. "I think it's a wonderful idea."

Relief and joy surged through him. He reached up, his hand cupping the back of her neck, drawing her down for a kiss that was slow, sweet, and full of a future he hadn't dared to dream of until her. It was a kiss that promised shared dawns, quiet evenings, and a lifetime of making a difference, side by side. A lifetime of sweet.

EPILOGUE

Jillian Sweet leaned back, surveying the scene spread out before her. Chores were done, the week was winding down, and the conversations flowed as easily as the sweet tea Alice kept refilling. Garret stood by the massive smoker wielding tongs with the authority of a pit master while the scent of burning mesquite and seasoned meats made her mouth water.

Across from her Rachel and Jim's shoulders brushed as they leaned in to share a quiet comment over something Mason explained with barbecue-sauce-covered hands. A moment after, the newly married couple shared a glance. The food forgotten, Jim sweetly swirled gentle caresses with his thumb along Rachel's arm. Her sister and her new husband radiated a quiet, confident happiness, a comfortable intimacy that made Jillian's heart feel a little lighter.

"Garret, these ribs are fantastic." From her seat at the picnic table under the massive oak, Sarah Sue licked sauce from her fingers.

"You outdid yourself with the brisket." Seated beside his wife, Carson stabbed at another slice, the two pausing to smile at each other as if their very lives depended on maintaining a silent connection.

"Honestly, Alice," Jess reached for another helping of potato salad, "what's your secret? Mine never, ever tastes this good, and I swear I follow your recipe to the letter."

A contented twinkle in her eye, their mother smiled. "My pinch may be bigger—or smaller—than yours. All you need is more practice. You'll get there."

The cheerful chatter around the table paused as Preston

pushed his chair back and stood. He caught Sarah Sue's eye, his hand finding hers for a brief, reassuring squeeze before he reached into his back pocket and pulled out a folded envelope. "Mom," his voice caught for a brief second, "this is for you."

Alice set down her fork, wiping her hands on a napkin before accepting the envelope. Brows furrowed, she pulled out the documents. With every scan of the papers, her eyes grew wider and wider. "Preston, what is this?"

"The docs—well, copies—from Dad's smallest loan." Preston's gaze remained fixed on his mother, a proud smile teasing the corners of his mouth. "And the notice from the bank that at least one loan is now paid in full."

Silence hung over the family meal. All eyes on their mother, her face transforming, when she looked up, tears shimmered in her eyes. "How?"

Preston casually hefted one shoulder. "We all contributed."

Glancing around the group, Jillian smiled at the quiet satisfaction on each face. At his grandmother's side, even young Mason seemed to understand something important was happening.

Her back straightening as their mother looked skyward, blinked, and an infectious grin took over her face, reaching eyes now sparkling with delight—and a little mischief. "Someone get me a match!"

Amidst the ensuing cheers and laughter, Carson produced a lighter. Soon, the paper—a symbol of so much struggle and effort—curled into ash in the fire pit normally used for S'mores and late-night ghost stories.

Couples fell into tender embraces, sharing gentle touches, before group hugs and high-fives added to the elation of the shared victory.

Just as the last embers of the loan papers died down, the distinct rumble of a heavy truck approached, growing louder, pulling everyone's attention away from the fire and toward the house.

Only one person didn't look confused at the sound.

Taking hold of Rachel's hand, Jim tugged her to her feet. "Perfect timing."

The two led the way to the front of the house as a flatbed truck rolled to a stop. On its bed, an impossibly shiny green, brand spanking new hay baler.

"You know about this?" Rachel spun around and stared up at her husband.

His smile wide, Jim nodded. "Slightly belated wedding gift," his voice came out soft but carried across the suddenly quiet group. "I figured it was time the Sweet Ranch had equipment that wouldn't break down every other week."

"It's too much." Rachel shook her head.

Carson, Preston, and Garret stood mesmerized as the driver hopped out of the truck.

"She's right." Preston sighed. "We can't let you—"

His hand up, palm out, Jim cut Preston off. "No argument. If any of you could have done this, you would have. This is for the ranch, the legacy we'll be giving our children."

While Jim may have been referring to the next generation in general, Rachel's cheeks blushed a light rose color as she leaned into his shoulder. He circled his arms around her, and she clung to him as if he'd just handed her the moon instead of a piece of farm machinery.

Her brother's gaze darted from one to the other, all the siblings, including Jillian, gave a curt nod. A silent agreement made that Jim, now part of the Sweet family, had every right to contribute as anyone else. The decision made, everyone crowded around the truck, talking over each other. Mention of horsepower and efficiency ratings tumbled over each other.

Standing slightly apart from the chaos, her sister's face tilted up toward her husband's, both wore expressions of such profound love and contentment that it made Jillian's heart swell. Most of her siblings had found that someone special. Had pulled together and not only made massive strides in saving their family legacy, but had found a love like their parents had shared, something that with each passing day, Jillian doubted would be her fate. At least not now. Now, her duty to the family was to find a husband and help pay off another loan. Too bad she didn't have a bloody clue where to find him.

Enjoy an excerpt from
Sweet Obsession

"Heads up!"

Jillian sprang back just as a hammer sailed through the air, landing a few inches in front of her.

"Sorry about that." Garret slid down a support post with the ease of a fireman gliding down a steel pole on his way to save lives. "I missed the loop in my belt. You okay?"

Nodding, she smiled at her brother. This wouldn't be the first or last time since the new construction project began that she'd been bumped, dinged, or suffered a near miss. She had the black and blues to prove it. "No harm, no foul."

Lips pressed tightly together, Garret nodded, and falling into place beside his sister, scanned the finally complete frame of what would soon be the Sweet Ranch's new calving barn. The foundation had been poured weeks ago, and now the wooden bones stretched skyward, outlining the structure that for so many years had lived only in their father's notes and dreams. "Dad would love it."

All the siblings who'd worked today gathered in a line and nodded their agreement.

Propped against a stack of lumber, music drifted from Preston's phone—a smooth blend of easy listening rock and country that made the assembly feel a little less like work and a little more like a party.

Alice, their mother, gazed across the burgeoning structure, a soft, approving smile on her face. "Charlie would be so proud."

"He really would." Garret eyed the scribbled notepaper

tacked to a center post. Their father had mapped out a plan and everyone felt a surge of pride at reaching another milestone on the long to-do list. "We've managed to get most of the pastures improved the way he wanted—organic fertilization, got a handle on the worst of the weeds, and Preston's rotational grazing system seems to be working wonders."

"And that new baler Jim bought has been a godsend." Carson hammered a stray nail flush. "We finally managed to acquire a few more head of cattle last month. Not as many as we'd hoped for initially, but it's a start. Should help with the income stream a bit."

Consulting his tablet where he'd been tracking their progress, Preston nodded. "If we can get this barn finished before calving season starts, we'll be in good shape. Thank God for Carson's construction connections—saved us a fortune on the foundation and framing."

Her head bobbing, Alice walked over to a plywood storage closet they'd built into one corner of the frame—a necessary precaution after the mysterious disappearance of the stolen hay baler they'd found hidden in the line shack. She carefully placed a set of new power tools inside. "Speaking of mysteries, any more news on Ray or those other hands?"

Preston shook his head. "Nothing solid."

A timer chimed from Alice's phone. "Oh, that's my roast. You all keep working—dinner in an hour." She hurried toward the house.

The moment their mom was out of earshot, Jillian spun around to face her brother. "So what aren't you telling us?"

Rubbing the back of his neck, Preston sighed. "Sean Farraday called earlier today. Told me he'd bumped into Ray—or someone who looked exactly like him—working for the Brady ranch near them."

"Mr. Farraday found Ray? Does the sheriff have him?" A million things swirled through Jillian's mind, the first being how she'd love to be back in the old west when they happily drew and quartered cattle rustlers. Or maybe it was just tarred and feathered. Either would do.

"'Fraid not. Sean didn't say anything, played it casual. The guy claimed his name was John Smith. By the time Sean got a hold of Declan, Ray and all his gear was gone."

"For a stellar thief, not a very original alias." Rachel rolled her eyes and shook her head.

"Wait." Carson's head snapped around. "Why was Ray working? That doesn't make sense at all."

"Agreed." Rachel joined them from where she'd been sorting lumber. "Considering how much money he must have squirreled away from everything he stole from us, why would he need to work at all? He should be on a beach in some country where he can't be extradited."

"If he's as smart as we thought, agreed." Preston shrugged again.

"Or he's lying low, trying to blend in," Garret suggested darkly.

"I'd like to stick with he's an idiot." Rachel flashed a fake smile. "Gives me hope we'll actually catch the S.O.B."

The conversation turned to their own finances—how much progress they'd made, but how far they still had to go. Jillian felt the familiar weight of expectation settling on her shoulders. Four siblings down, four successful marriages that had brought crucial trust fund payments. Now it was her turn.

Just then, the music from Carson's phone shifted. The twangy country faded, replaced by the soft, intricate fingerpicking of an acoustic guitar, a melody that was both melancholic and hopeful. A familiar male voice, rich and unexpectedly gentle, began to sing—one of Blake Kirby's older, lesser-known tracks, from before the stadium tours and the chart-topping anthems.

Garret paused. "That's a new one on Carson's playlist."

Looking up, Rachel stopped to listen. "Hard to believe that we knew Blake when he was nothing more than one of Kade's buddies. Who knew all that fiddling with the guitar would take him to the top of the charts?"

Now Garret stepped away from the storage closet, shaking his head. "Funny, isn't it? Buys that bazillion-dollar place down near the Austin music scene, supposedly to be closer to family, and yet he hasn't set foot back in Honeysuckle in years."

"Why should he come home?" Preston waved a hand at no one in particular. "He flies his family anywhere they want to see him on tour. From what I hear, his grandmother used to follow him around the country like a groupie."

That made Jillian chuckle. Sarah Kirby was as feisty as they come. The old woman would probably outlive them all and still be dancing after everyone was gone.

Carson heaved a sigh. "Can't blame him. It's certainly easier than dealing with grapevine queen Iris Hathaway."

Her brothers were right. This town held very little for Kirby. Only half-listening to the ongoing conversation, the music pulled her back to a memory from years ago. She was a little girl again, sitting off to the side on the back porch. Kade and his friends, Blake among them, playing a game of touch football on the sprawling back lawn. An idea had struck Blake, mid-play. He'd grabbed his battered guitar from the back of his pickup, settled onto the porch steps, and oblivious to the shouts and laughter around him, began to coax a new tune from the strings. Jillian had sat, mesmerized, as scattered notes bloomed into that unforgettable, haunting melody now playing from Carson's phone. When he'd finally looked up, his fingers stilling on the frets, and seen her sitting there, listening so intently, he'd smiled. She'd never forgotten that smile, the raw beauty of the tune, or the boy who'd become a rock star.

The song ended, and the usual country twang returned, snapping Jillian back to the present, the ranch, their dilemma, and the sound of a ticking clock in her head reminding her that her time to find a partner in crime was running out.

A galaxy of phone lights held aloft, the audience swayed dutifully as Blake played the last, fading note of the encore, "Honeysuckle Memories." With bittersweet lyrics about dusty roads and firefly nights, no one in this sprawling arena would likely understand the true origins. The applause washed over him, a familiar wave, warm and thunderous. The final show of a three-month tour, tonight the crowd had been electric—singing every word back to him.

He offered a practiced bow, called out a "Thank you, goodnight!" into the mic that would be broadcast onto the massive screens, and strode off stage right. The roar of the crowd, the chants of "Kirby! Kirby!" were already beginning to recede as he navigated the labyrinth of backstage corridors, the sudden shift to organized chaos a well-rehearsed dance.

This was it. End of the line for the "Wildfire" tour. Eighteen months, countless cities, and too many hotel rooms to count. He could already hear the pop of champagne corks from the band's dressing room down the hall; half of them were probably already making plans to celebrate with the usual entourage of hopefuls, industry hangers-on, and women whose names they wouldn't remember by morning.

He bypassed it all with a curt nod to Marcus, his perpetually harried tour manager, who was already barking into two phones at once, and a brief wave to Milo. Compact and surprisingly unassuming for a man who could probably disable three assailants before they hit the floor, his bodyguard fell into step a few paces behind, a silent, ever-present shadow.

The transition from stage god, commanding the attention of tens of thousands, to solitary man in a sterile black SUV was always jarring, the familiar post-show restlessness settling in. In the presidential suite of the five-star hotel, the silence shrouded him like a heavy blanket, broken only by the distant hum of city traffic twenty floors below. Ignoring the artfully arranged platter of gourmet snacks and the chilled champagne waiting on the coffee table, he walked to the panoramic window. The city lights spread out below him like a carpet of fallen stars, beautiful but impersonal. He'd seen a thousand cities like it. After a while they all blurred into one.

He ran a hand through his already disheveled hair. Sleep was a distant rumor. The adrenaline that had carried him through two and a half hours of performance was still a live current under his skin, thrumming with restless energy. He picked up his oldest, most battered acoustic—the one that had seen him through countless late nights in dingy college bars and even earlier, quieter nights on his grandmother's porch back in Honeysuckle. Its scarred wood felt more familiar, more real, than any of the high-end, custom-made instruments that now populated his collection.

His fingers found the strings, not with the practiced precision of his stage show, but with a hesitant, searching touch. A new riff, something softer than his recent chart topping hits, began to form under his restless touch. It was a wisp of a melody, something that had come to him unbidden, the way tunes used to arrive before writing music became a job, a product to be packaged and sold. This felt different, purer. He played it again, the notes hanging in the quiet air, more honest than anything he'd put on the last album.

Blake lost track of time as he worked through the progression, adding flourishes, finding the heart of the song that wanted to emerge. This was what he'd fallen in love with—not the screaming crowds or sold-out stadiums, but these quiet moments when music created itself through his hands.

The shrill ring of his phone cut through the melody, jarring him back to the present. Two in the morning. Who on earth…? He glanced at the caller ID, a frown creasing his brow. His grandmother. Sarah Kirby. A wave of affection, quickly followed by a prickle of unease, washed over him. Grams never called this late. Or for some, this early.

He swiped to answer, the new melody dissolving. "Grams?"

"Blake, darling!" Her voice, usually a warm, Texas drawl, sounded unusually bright, almost unnervingly chipper for what was nearly four in the morning Texas time.

"Is something wrong?"

"Of course not. I bet you thought I forgot, didn't you?"

"Forgot?"

"Your birthday."

Setting the guitar against the wall, Blake leaned back into the stiff hotel chair. "Birthday?" Maybe she was sleep calling, because he and she both knew his birthday was months away.

"A grandmother never forgets her favorite grandson's special day." He could hear the smile in her voice.

"Grams, I'm your *only* grandson."

"Pfft. That's semantics. You're still my favorite."

Despite his mounting confusion over this odd hour phone call, Blake found himself smiling. "You got me there, but why are you up at four in the morning?"

"Morning? It's the middle of the afternoon." Her tone shifted to one of admonishing adult. "I just had a cup of tea and wanted to call you before you thought I'd forgotten your special day."

They talked for a little longer, Grams chatting about neighbors and weather and asking about friends from high school he hadn't seen in close to a decade. When she finally said goodbye, claiming she needed to start dinner, he was left staring at his phone. What the heck was going on?

Sweet Obsession is available now

MEET CHRIS

USA TODAY Bestselling Author of dozens of contemporary novels, including the award winning Aloha Series, Chris Keniston lives in suburban Dallas with her husband, two human children, and two canine children. Though she loves her puppies equally, she admits being especially attached to her German Shepherd rescue. After all, even dogs deserve a happily ever after.

More on Chris and all her books can be found at
www.chriskeniston.com

Follow Chris' Monday Blog at her website
ChrisKenistonAuthor

Follow Chris on Facebook at
ChrisKenistonAuthor

Never miss a New Release!
Sign up for News from Chris:
www.chriskeniston.com/newsletter.html

Questions? Comments?
I would love to hear from you! You can reach me at:
chris@chriskeniston.com

www.ingramcontent.com/pod-product-compliance
Lightning Source LLC
Chambersburg PA
CBHW030005010826
48973CB00009B/2674